I0682486

DAVID GOLDON

Book one in the ENGLE BYEN series

ENGLE BYEN
A PLACE TO CALL HOME

SECOND EDITION
~ July 2018

Includes one ENGLE BYEN Short Story
and the first chapter of the Prequel:
THE ROAD TO ENGLE BYEN

DAVID GOLDON

DAVID GOLDON

SECOND EDITION
July 2018

First published in the USA in 2018
Printed and bound in the USA

ISBN: 978-0-6481954-3-6

Cover Image by www.SelfPubBookCovers.com/Viergacht

Contact: DavidGol**dd**on@gmail.com
www.DavidGoldon.com

Exclusive management, promotion and editing through:
AVA ORION Media
Melbourne, Australia

www.AvaOrionMedia.com

Editor, Proof-reader, Formatting &
Design: Michael Young
www.MichaelYoungAuthor.com

DAVID GOLDON

CONTENTS:

Continued over...

CONTENTS:

DAVID GOLDON

FOREWORD

The FIRE and WATER of creative flow is the balance that comes from two complementary natures.

Over a year ago I joined my author friend, Vicki Williams, as we began the Wyndham Writing Group in Werribee; west of Melbourne, Australia. What a wild ride it has been since then!

Initially, David came along to provide 'emotional support' as I took that next step in my writing journey that had already taken most of my adult life. Then, one winter's day, everything changed when we did an exercise using writing prompts and *everyone* in the room was encouraged to 'give it a go' and see what may happen.

With great resistance and complete self-doubt, David used a prompt to write a paragraph. After reading it out to the group, he was shocked to see the unanimous enthusiasm for what he had written. That very first piece he wrote has become the Prologue to this, his first novel. The rest is history.

As we publish ENGLE BYEN: A PLACE TO CALL HOME for the second time, David is writing book four in the ENGLE BYEN series, we are preparing book three to be published, and they just keep getting better! As his partner of 17 years, I am incredibly proud of him and to be a part of what we are creating together. I'm also jealous of how prolific he is, and I love him dearly... we are Fire and Water!

One day soon, this book and others will be filmed. I'm determined to see that happen because the world needs to experience the beauty and magic of the world he has created ... the town called ENGLE BYEN, a place we could all call home.

MICHAEL YOUNG
July 2018

AVA ORION Media

www.AvaOrionMedia.com

www.MichaelYoungAuthor.com

MichaelYoung3030@gmail.com

DAVID GOLDON

Book one in the ENGLE BYEN series

ENGLE BYEN
A PLACE TO CALL HOME

DAVID GOLDON

DAVID GOLDON

DEDICATION

I would like to dedicate, this, my very first story to my partner of seventeen years, Michael Young. He is my advisor, supporter, editor, proofreader and hand-holder through my first writing journey. I love you.
www.MichaelYoungAuthor.com

I would also like to thank Vicki Williams for the initial push to get me going and the continued support and guidance on this journey.
www.VickiWilliamsAuthor.com.au

DAVID GOLDON

Prologue:
Cold

A heavy mist encases me, limiting the view of my surroundings. I don't feel the cold biting chill that should accompany this dark, gloomy winter's day.

I make the same journey often, how often, I don't know, time is just a word. Something piques my curiosity in this unchanging environment; something appears different.

My eyes scan the area near me and as far into the distance as I can see. I don't notice anything different. In the dead quiet of this place, I hear the crunching of gravel, footsteps. The crunching noise becomes louder and closer.

I see two figures dressed in black, a male and a female walking towards me. Gradually, through the mist, I make out the faces of the approaching couple; it's mum and dad.

I give them a limp smile which isn't acknowledged as they stand either side of me.

Standing in between them, I wrap my arms around their waists, drawing them in closer to me. In unison, we lower our heads to view the cold grey marble headstone...

DAVID GOLDON

Chapter One:
Seachange

It was time for me to go.

I bought a large paper map, opened it up and laid it out on the table. I closed my eyes so tightly I could see specs of colours darting around. I raised my index finger above my head, waving it around like a magician waves a magic wand. Then I allowed my finger to hover over the map. As though it had developed a will of its own my finger came down firmly on a location on the map. It landed on the unusually named town of Engle Byen, and here I am.

I decided to move to Engle Byen without much thought. My old life was becoming confused. For the first time in my life, I wanted to run away; I needed to get away. Being a nurse means work is easy to come by and I knew I would find work wherever I ended up moving to.

Just like that, I packed up my old life and moved. Totally on a whim which was quite uncharacteristic for me. I felt like a magnetic force was dragging me away from my previous existence before something bad happened.

Engle Byen is a coastal town, overrun by tourists in the summer months and as autumn sets in, they all leave, and just the locals remain. This town is such a beautiful place to call home. The weather couldn't be more perfect. The days are bright and sunny; they fill me with happiness.

Just about every second house in my court location is empty at the moment as we head into autumn. I live in a lovely, newly renovated Californian bungalow style house. Being an organised person, all the boxes were quickly unpacked and the few sticks of furniture were neatly arranged in the appropriate rooms.

Even though I've only been living in this house six months, I've already accumulated twelve goldfish which were donated a few at a time, from various co-workers, who, rather than flush the sick fish down the toilet, gave them to me. I seem to have a knack for restoring sick animals back to health. Maybe I should've been a vet.

I do love my new position at St Angelina's hospital. Nursing is a rewarding career and looking after my patients is my top priority. Though the shift work can be a bit of a bummer, especially being new to the area, I'm eager to make some new friends.

I've met some of my neighbours; they're a mixed bunch. There's Gabriella who lives at No. 24; I have some suspicions about her. She's overly friendly, always waving and smiling at me when I jog past her house on the way to the park or the beach. I sense there's more to her than meets the eye. Something I can't quite put my finger on.

There's the lovely Muriel at No. 33 to my left. She also seems to spend a fair bit of time in her front yard. Broom in hand she sweeps the concrete path to her front door; her little white dog usually grabbing at the broom as she sweeps. Coincidentally, she was a patient of mine and we've become close quite quickly. I think it's because she found someone (me) to look after her from time to time.

Ralph lives beside me, we often have a chat over the side fence. I swear I saw him having a peek at me a few days ago through a hole in the old wooden fence when I was getting a bit of the last of the autumn sun in the backyard. I did give him a reason to be a peeping Tom; I was only wearing tiny football shorts. I like to keep trim and in shape and I look pretty good in the mirror, even if I do say so myself.

DAVID GOLDON

Chapter Two:
Crows

There was an odd sound coming from outside my bedroom window as I gradually woke from a deep sleep. The sun was beginning to rise and I heard the sound of crows calling out.

'Oh bugger, the damn crows are rummaging through my garbage bin,' I thought.

I jumped out of bed, threw on some clothes and headed for the front door. It was deadlocked.

'Damn, where are the keys?'

I headed to the back door to find the keys. I was relieved to see them in the lock. I could still hear the crows calling but they seemed louder, like they were on the other side of the back door. I unlocked the door, threw it open.

'No crows out here either.'

With keys in hand, I returned to the front door and walked outside. I saw the garbage bin with the lid still closed and not a crow to be seen. I made my way over to the garbage bin, my feet getting wet with morning dew as I crossed over the pavement. I inspected the lid; it was closed tight, no sign of crows anywhere.

'Maybe I heard their calls coming from a neighbour's house?'

"Good boy, it's alright, who's a good boy. I won't hurt you," I said to the big black dog that had suddenly appeared growling at me. I was trying to keep calm and not appear to be nervous even though I was shaking.

Animals and I have some type of affinity; they're never fearful of me nor me of them; they tend to be drawn to me, but not this dog! He just stayed there in front of me growling, kind of transfixed on me. Usually, Rottweilers are pretty scary looking but this one was a mean son of a...

"Cujo. Stay. Drop!" came a voice from behind me.

'Cujo? What? Really? You're kidding me! What a clichéd name for such a vicious dog like this one,' I thought. *'Calm down and pull yourself together Michael, situation under control.'*

Cujo did exactly as the voice asked. "Sorry about that, mate."

I turned around and saw the most beautiful looking man I'd ever seen. He was about the same height as me, six foot; lean build, thick black hair and a bit of scruff on his chiselled face.

He walked right up close to me. So close he was invading my personal body space. His eyes mesmerised me; they were the most beautiful shade of dark brown; his lips were full and luscious. My heart was pounding fast and my body began quivering. Not out of fear this time. I was totally consumed and enchanted by this guy's devilish good looks.

He was wearing a tight black polo top outlining his perfect pectorals and muscled biceps with a perfect amount of dark chest hair exposed around his neckline. If I could describe the perfect man, he was standing right here in front of me. Close. So close. Too close. I didn't hesitate to welcome him into my personal space.

Next thing I recall, "You alright mate? I'll call an ambulance," I heard him say as he picked me up off the wet, dew covered grass.

"No, I'm fine, I'm a nurse," I managed to say as I steadied myself into a standing position.

"How long was I out of it?" I asked.

"About six minutes. I was about to give you mouth to mouth but realised you were breathing."

'Damn!'

"I'm Jacob by the way, nice to meet you mate. I just moved into the area about six weeks ago. This guy you have already met, his name is Cujo."

'You may be the most handsome man I have ever met but you suck at naming your dog.'

"Michael. Likewise. Thanks for picking me up."

"Cujo! Home!" the handsome Jacob shouted at his big butch dog and off Cujo headed. I couldn't quite see which yard he went into but it must have been close. He disappeared just as fast as he had appeared scaring the life out of me.

"I haven't seen you around before, Michael. Are you new to the area?" Jacob asked.

"No. Well, I've been here for about six months, moved from interstate and just felt drawn to come to this area, and here I am. I work at St Angelina's as a nurse and do shift work so I'm in and out a bit."

A sly smile came over Jacobs's handsome face. "I used to come here on holidays with my parents when I was younger; they owned the house that I live in now. They both passed away several years ago. I inherited the holiday house and let it sit empty for a while so now I'll probably live in it for a bit. I'll keep an eye out for you. We should get together and hang out a bit if you're up for it?" Jacob said in a flirtatious manner.

"Yeah, that'll be great," I replied with a stammer.

'*How embarrassing*,' I thought as I walked back up the three wet steps into my house. He had me stumbling over my words. I hope he didn't notice.

I went directly to the bathroom and looked in the mirror; I looked a mess. I had bed hair but at least my bright, ice blue eyes weren't all crusty. I must admit though, I do cut a decent figure in the tight t-shirt and tracky dacks that I was wearing.

Then I recalled why I went outside in the first place; it was in search of the noisy crows.

'*What is it they call a group of crows? Ah yes; a murder.*'

Chapter Three:
Gabriella

"Oh yeah, that's it. Go harder, even harder. I can take it. A bit to the left. A bit more. No, over to the right, almost, yeah, just there." I gave out a painful moan to my massage therapist.

As you age, I guess your body starts to fall apart; well that's what's been happening to me for the past six months. My twenty-nine-year-old shoulders are in constant pain but not enough to keep me from working at St Angelina's.

"Oh yeah, that's it. Keep working on that spot," I continued.

"Michael, you know, you really should be having that x-ray I mentioned to you two sessions ago. Those slight lumps are still on your shoulder blades," said Viktor.

Viktor looks like your typical Swedish backpacker type; young, a stylish quiff of blond hair, blue eyes, tanned and toned. He's in town on a twelve-month working holiday. I've been lucky enough to have him as my in-house masseur at the hospital. He's gorgeous, always flirting with me and that sexy Scandinavian accent melts me to the core. Even though we've only recently met, I feel as though I've known him all my life; there's a strange yet warm familiarity about him.

"Michael, your legs are like tree trunks," he complimented me.

"That's because I'm Sagittarian, Viktor. You know, half man half horse."

"Oh, I know which half is the horse," Viktor giggled. "Are you dating anyone yet, Michael? Because you know I am free and single and ready to mingle," Viktor said in his gorgeous accent.

"Sorry Viktor, professional boundaries and all."

"So, happy ending then, Michael?"

We burst into hysterical laughter.

* * *

I could hear opera music blasting out as I walked up the front steps. "Come in darling, come in," a husky voice called out in a theatrical, over the top tone.

"Oh, my darling Michael. Champagne dear? I have some on ice. Also, two gorgeous crystal flutes are just crying out in anticipation to be filled to overflowing with tiny bubbles." Gabriella swanned over to her already open front door. She was wearing a bright copper coloured kaftan, which flowed as she floated seamlessly to the door and welcomed me in.

She air-kissed me on both cheeks and ruffled my hair while her gold bangles jingled and jangled down her arms. As I walked in past her, she grabbed my butt cheeks and gave them a firm squeeze.

"Hmmm, firm and ripe darling, and so pert. Must be all that physical activity you do. I see you running most days in those tiny shorts. Legs like tree trunks, too delicious for words."

'The neighbours don't miss anything around here,' I thought as I felt my face turn slightly red.

Gabriella's house is in the same style as all the rest in our court, a Californian bungalow. Inside, her decorating style is perhaps quite eclectic and not to my taste at all. Her living room is filled with old movie posters adorning the walls, brightly coloured stain glass lamps all over the place, metres of different types of fabrics draped over chairs, and the smell of sage fills the room.

"Sit, sit," she beckoned me flapping her wrinkly, large hands over in the direction of a three-seater lounge. I sat down as she swanned her way into the kitchen. I haven't been in her house before although we've chatted in the street a few times. It was on one of those occasions she told me she was a psycho, no *psychic*, and offered to give me a free reading. So there I was in the somewhat clichéd surroundings of someone who talks to the "other side".

Gabriella emerged from the kitchen with a classic silver champagne bucket with a bottle of her finest champagne on ice.

"Oh darls, how did you know? My favourite champagne," I cooed.

She winked and smiled at me, her heavy makeup cracking, almost falling off her face and revealing what looked like a five o'clock shadow. Nothing was subtle about Gabriella; she was quite tall, aged at least sixty years old, had short, scraggy, bleached blonde hair bordering on yellow; obviously looking like a cheap dye job.

She returned to the kitchen and emerged with two beautiful looking amethyst crystal champagne flutes and sat them down on the coffee table. A dignified slight 'pop' could be heard as she released the cork from the bottle and proceeded to pour the gorgeous bubbles into the flutes.

"Bottoms up," she cackled as the bubbles gently tickled my nose as I took a sip. "Now, what would you like my darling Michael?" she whispered seductively.

"Oh, I do love salmon dip. Bet you don't have that though, Gab?"

"Well, darling, if you look on the side table to your right."

'Well, blow me down, salmon dip, there it is!'

"Gabriella, how did you know?"

"It's my job to know these things; I am a physic extraordinaire after all. Now let's get on with your reading, shall we?"

She reached for my hands and held them firmly in hers. She looked deep into my eyes and I felt her bright blue eyes intensely staring right into, through and beyond my eyes; like into my soul or something.

Looking into her eyes, I felt I could see something like the whole universe, Earth, seas and land. It was weird.

'Champagne on an empty stomach was probably not a good idea.'

She broke eye contact and began caressing my hands which creeped me out.

'Has she drugged the champagne? I don't know her that well. Shit, shit, shit! I'm going to wake up with one kidney missing!'

She let go of my hands and those large talons of hers reached and grabbed the angel cards from the coffee table. She offered them to me. "Shuffle, darling, shuffle."

As I reached to take the cards from her, they flew up into the air and all fell face down on the dirty carpet.

'Exactly how much champagne did I have?'

"Alright, reading over darling. I'm feeling quite tired now, you'd better go." And with that, she pretty much pushed me out the door.

DAVID GOLDON

Chapter Four: Ralph

I could hear what sounded like a power drill. A strong, bright light shone in my face. I had a painful piercing sharp pain in my head.

'*Where am I, what's going on*?' I thought.

Then, suddenly, I sprang up out of my sleep.

'*Huh, what's that noise? Drilling? Where's it coming from?*'

I realised I'd nodded off while enjoying catching a few rays of this lovely warm and sunny autumn day. I rose slowly from my daybed and looked around the backyard. I took a few steps over to where the drilling noise was coming from. Feeling a slight breeze where there shouldn't be one, I realised I was au naturale. I quickly took a few steps backwards, grabbed my shorts and pulled them on. Beads of sweat dripped down my muscular chest. I grabbed a towel and dried myself off.

The drilling noise stopped and as I stood motionless, expecting it to start again; it didn't.

"Oh fuck!" I screamed out in shock as a head popped up from the other side of the fence. It was Ralph.

"Sorry Michael, did I scare you? I didn't think you were home."

'*Then why are you looking over my fence?*'

Ralph is about forty-five years old, quite handsome looking; I think he would have been a catch back in the day. He seems to spend his days gardening. His front yard is immaculately presented; I've often admired it as I pass by on my daily run. Ralph mostly keeps to himself. I don't know that much about him as we only have a general chat over the fence now and then. He lives alone.

I think he's hiding something. Just a feeling I get. Probably nothing, I know, but the stories he tells me about his life don't make sense. It feels like he makes things up as he goes along. Perhaps he's a compulsive liar, or maybe he's not quite right in the head. Anyway, he seems pleasant enough and he has a nice calm aura about him.

"What are you up to over there, what's all that drilling noise I can hear?" I tersely asked him.

"Oh, just a bit of work in the garden, you know. You seen that Jacob guy?" he asked, quickly changing the subject.

"Yes. Do you know him?"

"You keep away from that one. Nothing but trouble, you mark my words," Ralph warned, while his eyes were leering at my crotch.

'Ralph sounds like he's an eighty-year-old man,' I had a little giggle to myself.

"Oh really Ralph, and why is that?" I ask like a petulant child.

"He used to come up here with his parents on holiday every year. He was actually born in that very same house. His grandparents were locals here and they owned that house until they passed. Jacob's family used it as a holiday house every year since. Nothing but trouble that one."

"Thanks for the warning, Ralph; but you gotta give me something. You can't just tell me to keep away from him and not give me a reason."

I felt like Ralph was on the verge of telling me something about Jacob. It looked as though he was about to say it. He looked around him and then up to the sky before focusing his eyes on me again.

He fell silent and so I took my cue from that and simply replied, "I'll take care should I see him again."

Ralph's head descended behind the fence.

'Perhaps another time he'll spill the beans and tell me whatever this dark secret is that he's keeping to himself. Or maybe he's really into Jacob and wouldn't be able to cope if the most handsome man in Engle Byen went after me instead of him.'

DAVID GOLDON

Chapter Five: Jacob

Beep-beep, beep-beep, beep-beep...

I woke up suddenly and sat bolt upright in my bed.
'What's that sound? Sounds like a patient's heart rate monitor at the hospital. Am I at work, where am I?'

Regaining my senses, I recognised my surroundings.

'Oh okay, I'm at home in bed, must be the dishwasher finishing its load. Now I'm awake I may as well get out of bed.'

It was 9am and no work that day, so I thought I would go for a run. I slipped on some shorts, a singlet and my super new running shoes, and off I headed.

The morning sun was bright, the birds were singing, it was just another awesome autumn day in Engle Byen.

"Hey, Ralph," I called out as I ran past his house. "Looking good there Gabriella. See you this arvo, Muriel."

'All the neighbours are out, so friendly. I love my new life,' I thought to myself as I embarked on my 5km run.

* * *

Huffing and puffing, I reached my destination and headed for the water fountain in the park facing the coastal foreshore. I began guzzling the water. It was so refreshing and cooling, perfect. Boy, I was feeling hot, so I took off my singlet and headed to the bench seat overlooking the ocean.

There was a slight breeze which helped me get my body temperature back down. I did some stretches in preparation for my run back home. Then I decided to sit down for a while to admire the ocean view before heading off again.

"Oh shit!" I yelled out and jumped to my feet. I felt a hand tightly grip my right shoulder.

"Mate, so jumpy."

I turned around and there was a smiling Jacob. He was so damn good looking and not wearing a shirt! I hadn't seen him shirtless before and what an eyeful he was. Well-defined muscular chest lightly covered in hair, flat stomach, broad shoulders and pale skin. My eyes were scanning every inch of his body.

'Did I even look him in the eyes? Oh shit, Michael, look him in the eyes, and control yourself.'

"Do you come here often?" I asked.

'Oh, dickhead, Michael. What a lame thing to say.'

Jacob laughed. "First time in a while, I'd forgotten how beautiful this spot is. Mind if I sit?"

'Oh, you can sit on me anytime,' I naughtily thought. *'Focus, Michael.'*

As Jacob made his way to sit beside me on the bench, I could see his eyes slowly scanning my body. He was studying my chest, stomach, lingering a while on my crotch and then slowly eyeing my legs all the way down.

"We have quite similar bodies, Michael; except those legs of yours they look like tree trunks."

'Hmmmm, he certainly made no secret of checking me out.'

"There's a gym at the hospital where I work, so I go there. I love to run on days like this when the weather is perfect."

Jacob looked around; there was no one around but an old couple walking hand in hand on the beach in the distance. He placed his hand on my leg and kept it there for around thirty seconds.

'A little too long, oh shit, shit, shit, he's coming onto me!'

"Well, Michael, I'm going to wash the sand off me before I go home. Do you want a lift?"

"Uh-no, thanks," I said in a little too quickly, "I'll run home."

With that, Jacob gave me a devilish bad boy grin and walked over to the outdoor shower and turned the water on. I watched him glance back over to me before taking his swim shorts off revealing black swimming briefs and something rather large bulging from them as the water cascaded down his perfect body.

I stood up once my own excitement settled down, gave him a wave and started the run back home. Boy, did I run!

'I'm not sure what it is about Jacob. Usually, if someone is giving me all the signals, which I'm sure he is, I would've taken them up on the offer.'

All that was going through my mind as I continued running home.

Once home I opened the front door, stripped off and headed straight for a cold shower!

Though I was used to getting a lot of attention, with Jacob, it was different.

'I want him, but I don't. Why?'

Chapter Six:
Muriel

Buzz Buzz, Buzz; Text message coming through.

'*Who can this be?*'
I reached and looked at the message on my phone. It was Muriel.
'*What does she want now,*' I wondered as I opened the message.

She wanted me to pick up some groceries for her at the supermarket

I replied that I'd do that for her and drop them off after work tonight. She responded as usual with a 'thank you' and that I was an angel.

Now, I don't mind helping others, but some people can be particularly needy. Muriel and I did form a close bond when I was nursing her back to health at St Angelina's. Little did I know she was living in my street and her attachment to me has grown stronger. I did read out the 'patient/nurse professional boundaries warning' to her before her discharge, but she wouldn't have any of it and, me being the caring, compassionate fool that I am, I stepped over those boundaries as well.

Muriel lives in an older, un-renovated Californian bungalow house with her little mixed breed, white, furry dog called Fluffy.

'*Oh please, really, Fluffy? How original. Not!*'

She doesn't have any relatives that I know of, and no one comes to visit her, so I know she appreciates my time. She spends most of her day painting, drawing, sculpting; all manner of creative arts.

She gave me a painting of an angel that she'd done, it was really quite beautiful. The angel was a bare-chested guy with huge white wings. I got the luck of the draw with that one as most of her works are, well, they look like a child created them. I'm guessing she didn't actually paint the angel herself.

* * *

The barking started as soon as I opened Muriel's front gate. Fluffy was such a yappy thing, he was always happy to see me, and scratched my legs with his nails as he kept jumping up on me.

"Muriel, it's Michael. I've got the groceries you asked for!" I yelled. "Where's mummy, Fluffy?"

"Oh, Michael, you're an angel, always so reliable and helpful to an old girl like me," Muriel's voice rang out from inside her house. I opened the beautiful old wooden fly screen door and stepped in while rubbing the pain in my legs where Fluffy had scratched them up some.

"Oh look at you, legs like tree trunks," Muriel said.

I rarely raise my voice but couldn't help myself this time...

"Why the hell does everyone keep saying that to me, like you are all hinting at something, is there something weird about my legs Muriel? Go on tell me. Why tree trunks? Why do you all keep saying that? Why not strong, thick, muscular legs? That sounds better, but no, you all say the same thing, everyone, the exact same thing! You, Gabriella, Ralph, Viktor and then this morning, Jacob!"

"Jacob? Is he back in town?" Muriel asked quizzically, then she became unusually quiet. "You keep away from him, you hear? Never let him in your house and definitely not into your heart."

Muriel said it in a way that sounded much like a warning, really direct and to the point, it kind of scared me.

"Okay, you're the second person that's warned me off him, Ralph has as well. What's the story, is he like a vampire or something?" I giggled.

"Now, Michael, you know I don't speak unkindly of others, so I can't tell you the reason for my warning. You will have to figure it out yourself. Remember, there are always choices to be made, think carefully. If something is too good to be true, proceed with caution and most of all trust in yourself. Search for answers inside yourself; your spirit will guide you."

"Whoa, Muriel, where did all that come from?"

I noticed Muriel's face and demeanour had changed; she seemed to glow, shine, appear larger. I started to see little stars as my eyes shifted around. I tried to steady what I was seeing by trying to draw my gaze away from her and onto her questionable artwork on the walls.

My head became lighter and I was feeling dizzy. I tried to speak. I was slurring whatever I was trying to say. My shoulder blades began hurting quite badly.

'Must get back to Viktor, must have that x-ray we keep talking about.'

My head was pounding. The room went dark...

"Oh, Jacob, that feels amazing!" I moaned as he licked my neck. I whirled in this amazing feeling of ecstasy. I had finally succumbed to Jacob's evil bad-boy ways.

'What am I thinking, how did I let it get this far?'

His tongue began to explore my mouth. I felt waves of intense pleasure that I had never known before.

"Fluffy! Get off him!" Muriel shouted.

I woke up.

"What the...? Get that fucking dog off me!" I yelled. "Yuck! Gross! Muriel, what the hell happened?"

"You blacked out and fell to the floor."

"How long was I out for?" I demanded to know.

"About six minutes."

'Okay, Michael, calm down and don't blame Fluffy, it's not his fault.'

Then I recalled the fantasy I just had about Jacob; he was getting into my head, consuming my every thought.

Chapter Seven:
Mr Burgess

My alarm clock made an awful sound as it woke me up this morning.

'Must be the batteries going flat. No, hang on, it's electric, isn't it?'

My train of thought was interrupted when, out of the corner of my eye, I saw a large single white feather on the floor near my bed.

'That's odd, how did that get there?'

I got out of bed and picked it up; it was a beautifully clean white firm feather about six inches long.

'I think that's a good luck symbol or something. I must find out.'

I placed the feather on my bedside table, excited about what type of good luck would be coming my way and proceeded to get ready for my day shift at work.

* * *

"Michael, it's mum."

"Hi, Mum, how are things?"

"Michael, it's mum, can you hear me?"

"Yes Mum, I can hear you. Can you hear me?" Silence...

'Damn mobile coverage; I'll have to call her on the landline at work when I have a minute. She just can't grasp texting or email, she prefers the old-fashioned way

where you actually talk to someone, but at this rate, we'll never get to have a chat.'

* * *

Day shifts at work are usually super busy, and today was no exception. I work on ward six.

St Angelina's isn't a huge hospital, just big enough to cope with the number of patients we receive from this small town and the surrounding areas. There are generally three nurses on ward six for the day shift and just the one nurse for the night shift. There are also a few doctors coming and going. We have one admin person and one new orderly I haven't met yet. The ward is divided up between the private patient rooms and the public rooms, basically, the haves and the have-nots.

"Hey you, nurse man, get over here!" A call came out from one of the private rooms as I was walking past. It was Mr Burgess.

Mr Burgess has been admitted with stage three cancer and has chosen to spend his last days here at St Angelina's in a beautiful private room, well 'suite' really. The suite is beautifully appointed with large windows that overlook the ocean, a large overstuffed lounge and accompanying chairs, magazines and books neatly stacked on the glass coffee table. You wouldn't know you were actually in a hospital except for the machines and oxygen outlets near the over-sized bed.

Mr Burgess hasn't had any visitors that I knew of. He's a cantankerous, seventy-year-old so and so. He made his fortune on the stock market and various other entrepreneurial ventures. All we can do is make him as comfortable as possible and put up with all his nonsense. He loves to give us nurses a difficult time, so we try not to go into his room unless we really have to.

I popped my head into the room. "Yes, Mr Burgess, is there something wrong?" I asked.

"Where's that hot looking young orderly gone? She said she would drop by this morning to get my answer on something we discussed, well I have my answer. So where the hell is she?" he asked, getting quite agitated.

"She had an amazing sounding deal for me to consider purchasing from her," he continued. "It would revolutionise the IT industry. I went over the proposal she brought into me and I figured I could make a fortune from this. I do realise that I probably won't be around to see the huge financial windfall I can make from this, but I don't care. Whatever it takes to make loads of money, I'm in!

"She said this deal would come at a high price, but I'm the only guy around that can make this project a reality. So I says: 'Yeah, babe, count me in, I'd even sell my soul to the devil to make this thing happen.' Jacquie just laughed and said: 'Great, consider your soul mine. Sold!'

"My name will be on everybody's lips. I will be rich and famous and probably too dead to know about it. Just think of the legacy I'll be leaving the world, Burgess Electronics Inc. You can tell all your mates you knew me, the great and amazing business mogul; Angelo Burgess."

Finally, I got a word in, "Sorry, I don't know who Jacquie is, the orderlies rarely set foot into the patient's rooms or wards. We don't have any female orderlies that I know of on this ward, Mr Burgess. Are you sure it wasn't a nurse?"

"No! No, she was definitely an orderly, different uniform boy; I ain't losing my marbles yet!" he barked at me gruffly.

While I was checking his chart, I noticed a 'do not resuscitate' instruction.

'The grumpy old so and so must be on his way out. So rich and no freaking manners. He's been giving me a hard time for the last few days, probably because he knows he's not long for this world.'

"You have a good day now Mr Burgess," I said sarcastically. I snapped his chart shut loudly startling him and returned it to the foot of the bed. I left him in his private room to wait for the so-called female orderly.

Chapter Eight: Gym

I swiped my security card, *beep*!

The door to the men's locker room opened. I made my way to my locker and opened it. After a hard days work involving bedpans, sponge baths, catheters and the demanding Mr Burgess, I was relieved to begin to change out of my nurses uniform into my gym gear. I bent over to pick up my water bottle that dropped on the floor.

"What the hell!" I yelled out as I heard a loud metallic bang above my head which startled me. I looked up to see a hospital orderly with his hand on the front of my locker door.

"What the hell do you think you're doing? You scared the shit out of me!" I shouted at him as I stood to attention.

"Oh, you are bloody kidding me!" I exclaimed as my eyes focused on the perpetrator's face. Jacob.

"Hey there Michael, I was wondering when I was going to bump into you, and here you are."

"Jacob, nice to see you," I said.

'Well, it was always nice to see him. Who could resist that gorgeous face? Oh yeah, me, I keep resisting!'

I was also getting a bit creeped out because everywhere I went he appeared as if out of thin air. I didn't even hear him come into the locker room and I was the only one in there.

"Judging by the uniform, I gather you are working here now Jacob?"

"Yeah, well, I'm planning on staying in Engle Byen for a while so thought I'd get a job to help out with the bills and so on. Then I remembered you said you worked here, so I applied for an orderly position. I'm good handling stiffs." He smirked.

"I'm just about to hit the gym, it's in the basement downstairs," I said dismissing his crude comment.

"Cool, headed there myself. If you want to wait here while I get changed, I'll join you. It'll be awesome to have a gym buddy."

I noticed the name on his hospital ID badge; 'Jacob Devlin'.

'Hhhhmmm, so that's his last name.'

I walked over to the water fountain to fill up my drink bottle as Jacob was getting changed. I just knew he would be putting on another near naked display in front of me like he did when we met at the beach last time. I must admit I quite enjoyed it, but I was at work now.

"Okay mate, ready for our workout?" Jacob called across the locker room.

We made our way to the elevator to go the two floors down to the basement where the gym was located. Jacob walked out of the elevator first, and I couldn't help but notice his strong, muscular, hairy legs and bubble butt highlighted by the tiny shorts he was wearing.

'Focus, Michael!'

"Well, Jacob, this is St. Angelina's hospital gym! It's not that big but, being staff, it doesn't cost us anything to use. Let me show you around. There's a few machines over there, free weights near the male change rooms and here in the change rooms, as you can see, the open showers, soap dispensers next to the shower taps and towels are provided over by the vanity basins. Any questions?"

"Nope, all good thanks Michael. Let's get pumping."

We walked over towards the free weights and did a few stretches together. I was most impressed by all the muscles I could see in Jacob's back protruding from the skimpy singlet he was wearing.

"Spot me mate?" Jacob said as he headed to the bench press.

"Sure," I replied.

Jacob weighted up the barbell and laid down on the bench; I stood behind him. His head was positioned directly below my crotch. I felt slightly uneasy. He lifted up the barbell with more weight than I could ever lift. I assisted him easing down the barbell with every repetition, as a good spotter does. It wasn't long before I caught him looking up my shorts before each lift.

"Okay, your turn," he said to me. I began to take some of the weights off the barbell.

"No mate, leave them on, you can do it. I'm here to help you in any way I can."

Jacob took up the spotter's position behind me. I lay down on the bench and gripped the barbell. When I looked up, my eyes had no choice but to look directly above, right up and into Jacob's shorts. I couldn't help but notice he was commando!

'How am I going to concentrate now?'

He was right though; I didn't have any trouble lifting the weights up, I felt like I had acquired some superhuman strength.

"See mate, knew you could do it."

"Yeah, well thanks, I did, didn't I?" I responded sheepishly.

We took our time and continued for a few more sets. There was no one else in the gym; it doesn't tend to get used a lot.

"Mate, I'm so hot and sweaty," Jacob said leering at me. "Let's hit the showers?"

'*Oh no, no, no,*' I thought in a moment of rare self-restraint.

"I might just head home actually, it's getting a bit late," I told him.

"I could do with a lift mate. Do you mind hanging around a bit? I had to get the bus here today."

"Um, okay then, I can wait I guess. I'll just hang around in here and tidy up the weights while you shower."

"Cool mate, I won't be long, saves me some money on my water bill," he smiled.

As Jacob headed off to the change room, I had a last peek at his awesome physique. I went about picking up some weights and putting them back on the stands.

From the men's change room, I could hear the water from the shower. I was imagining Jacob standing there in all his glory, water cascading down that muscular torso, making its way, all the way, down his body.

I caved and immediately made my way into the change room. My heart raced as I slowly poked my head around the corner into the open shower area.

There he was, better than I had imagined. He was lathering himself up, paying particular attention to that python of his.

I felt like I was about to faint. The whole scene was too hot.

'You know you can have him. He virtually offered himself to you so what are you waiting for? Oh, Michael, what's wrong with you, you're obviously lusting after him so why are you resisting temptation? This is not like you.'

There was just something, something I couldn't quite put my finger on. I was so attracted to Jacob, yet I wasn't.

'He doesn't talk much, doesn't have a sense of humour, seems a bit serious, and there's always that strange sense of real danger when I look into his eyes.'

"Michael, nearly done," Jacob called out looking directly at me.

'Oh fuck, fuck, fuck,' I was busted.

DAVID GOLDON

Chapter Nine:
Take-out

We called in for some Chinese food to-go on the short trip home in my car. We decided to have dinner at my place, then Jacob could walk a few houses down to his home. No doubt his dog, Cujo, would be eagerly awaiting his master's return.

Jacob didn't say much as we drove to my house. He seems to be the quiet, brooding, bad boy type. My type which, I must say, gets me really hot.

'Michael, throw caution to the wind. Just give into temptation, go to the dark side, tonight's the night. Your now insatiable desire to bed this hot muscular stud can't wait any longer. Give in.'

I pulled into my driveway, got out of the car. I walked ahead of Jacob and opened my front door, flicking on the lights as I walked toward the kitchen. I turned around, no Jacob. I walked back to the front door, he was standing outside holding the plastic bags containing our dinner.

"Well, aren't you going to invite me in?" he asked.

"Um... yes, Jacob, you are invited to come in, please come in," I said in an overly formal but joking manner. He entered my home, his shoes making a clomping sound on the timber floorboards as he made his way to the kitchen.

I stood numb and frozen at the front door as I heard Muriel's voice going through my head; "*You keep away from him, you hear? Never let him in your house and definitely not into your heart."*

'*Oh shit, shit, shit and shit!!*' I thought in a panic. '*Why did he stand there outside the front door and ask to come into my house like that?*'

Then I recalled, '*Everyone knows a vampire has to be invited in, oh shit! Oh, that's it, he's going to bite my neck and drain me of my blood, he is a goddamn vampire! Do I have any garlic, what about a crucifix, a wooden stake, do I have a wooden stake to kill him with? What have I done!!*'

I was in such a panic; my mind was whirling around not knowing what to do next.

"Mate, are you expecting someone else? You've been standing there for a while, I've already plated up our dinner. You got any wine?"

"Oh yeah, sorry, I'm coming," I responded nervously.

As I walked down the passageway to the kitchen, I looked at the illuminated fish tank and noticed all the goldfish have congregated into the far corner, which was unusual; they're normally in the nearest corner waiting for some food.

In the kitchen, the dinner was all plated up and ready to eat.

"White or red wine, Jacob?"

"Red thanks," he replied.

I poured him a red and myself a white. Red goes straight to my head and I had to keep my wits about me in readiness for his fangs to appear.

I handed Jacob his glass of red.

"Look at that colour; it's a beautiful blood red," he said.

I nearly fainted. I took my plate and glass of wine and sat on the sofa. I ushered Jacob to do the same and he sat right next to me, his leg touching mine

'At least I'll make a hot looking vampire after he bites me!' I thought, having still not changed out of my gym clothes, and trying to distract myself with a bit of humour.

"Do the Chinese use garlic in their food?" I asked Jacob.

"Don't think so mate, ginger probably."

'Keep calm Michael, no such thing as vampires,' I remind myself. *'Calm down, idiot!'*

I'd lost my appetite. I had a little nibble of my dinner then remembered something.

"Back in a minute," I said to Jacob as I placed my plate down on the coffee table. In a panic, I walked really fast to the bathroom. I opened the cupboard and there it was; a little mirror.

'Uh-ha, you are so clever, Michael, everyone knows a vampire has no reflection in a mirror.'

I smirked, realising I had the upper hand on him.

Racing back to the lounge room, mirror in hand, I stood in front of Jacob with my back to him. I held the mirror up discretely. I could see myself and also Jacob, I was relieved he wasn't a vampire after all.

Taking a deep breath, I sat down.

"Mate, you alright?" this non-vampire asked me.

"Better than you could imagine, Jakey," I said in a relaxed manner.

'Oops, Jakey? Oh, shit. Hope he didn't hear that.'

"Jakey?" Jacob asked.

'Damn, bugger, shit, shit! He did hear me!'

I just ignored him.

"Oh, are we having pet names for each other, Mikey?" Jacob asked in a baby voice.

'Mikey, Mikey.' The name started to whirl in my mind.

'Mikey.' I kept hearing it.

'Sounds familiar but no one calls me that. Do they? Why is it resonating with me now? Bloody wine!'

I took another gulp knowing no vampire would be making a meal of me tonight. My mind came suddenly back into focus when Jacob placed his large, manly hand on my leg.

"Oh, look at the time," I said acting surprised. Jacob turned and looked me deep in the eyes. His eyes, dark; the darkest shade of brown I'd ever seen, almost black. Deliciously black, soulless, dead, lost, dangerous and yet confused. I was reading a lot from his eyes. I'd never looked so deep into them nor he into mine.

We broke eye contact as he stood up.

"Well, guess I better leave then," Jacob said despondently.

I also stood up from the sofa, a little wobbly from the wine, and escorted Jacob down the passageway to the front door.

Jacob was directly behind me when I reached out my arm to unlock the front door. Jacob firmly grabbed my arm, spun me around and pushed me up against the wall. His arm was firmly across my chest. I was a little shocked but also excited as Jacob's masculinity took over.

"Can we stop playing games?" he said in a hushed, gentle voice. "I can't make it any more obvious Michael.

I want you. I want to kiss those amazing lips of yours, caress your toned muscular body, wake up with you in the morning; together we can fly."

While still gently pinning me against the wall he slowly licked my lips with his tongue. His breath carried the scent of red wine. I could taste remnants of the wine as his tongue ever so slowly began exploring my mouth. I froze.

'Should I kiss him back? Oh, what the heck!'

I allowed my tongue to mingle with his, together they intertwined. He slowly slid his tongue out of my mouth, looked into my eyes and gave me a heart melting devilish grin. My heart began pounding relentlessly. I felt my cheeks redden. My breathing became short and shallow.

Jacob's arm released me from the wall while he pressed his body against mine. He kept my back firmly against the wall while his hands reached up under my singlet. Slowly rubbing my firm muscular chest, his hands made their way slowly over my nipples. He rubbed his warm hands feverishly over them as they stood to attention.

I let out a slight moan as I could feel Jacob's manhood harden as he pressed it firmly against mine. His hands lowered from my chest, explored my v-line then round to the small of my back. Slightly lifting the elastic of my shorts and underwear, he slipped his hands onto my butt. He kneaded and clenched my butt cheeks with his fingers. He began licking my neck up and down ever so slowly. The sensation sent pulsating chills all over my body. Pinned against the wall, I didn't resist.

I was blissfully being transported somewhere else when a horrible thought crossed my mind...

'Fluffy!'

I had a flashback to the last time Jacob was sending me into ecstasy, and when I came to from one of my blackouts, I found Muriel's dog, Fluffy, not Jacob, licking me.

"Get the fuck off me Fluffy!" I yelled as I pushed Jacob off me. His hands came out from the back of my shorts. The look on his face was less than pleased.

"What the hell Michael!"

I snapped out of it.

'Okay, this is real, me in my house kissing Jacob.'

Muriel's warning about Jacob was again replaying through my mind, *"You keep away from him. You hear? Never let him in your house and definitely not into your heart."*

I'd already broken the do-not-let-him-in-your-house warning, nothing bad happened, in fact, he was the best kisser ever!

'Should I heed Muriel's warning? Well, the second bit at least. In a few moments, he will be in my bed.'

The door slammed shut.

'Guess that's my mind made up then,' I realised as Jacob vanished behind the door.

'This has been a long night.'

Before retiring to bed, I tidied up the kitchen and began turning off lights. As I reached to turn off the fish tank light, six of the twelve goldfish were floating on the surface of the water. Dead.

Chapter Ten:
Dream

Bang! Bang! Bang!

I woke up suddenly from my deep sleep; my head was pounding. I must have been suffering the effects of last night's dream.

'Or was it a nightmare?'

It starts off quite nicely. I'm trying to fly. I'm running down my street on a beautiful sunny day, flapping my arms like they are wings. Eventually, I take off and fly for a little bit, then come back down to the ground. I continue running and fly up again for a short while and back down again. I often have this type of dream, nothing unusual there.

'Maybe they're trying to tell me something?'

However, in last night's dream, giant pure white wings explode out of my back. It hurts at first then the pain numbs, and I'm overwhelmed with an incredible feeling of peace and freedom. I'm wearing white linen trousers, no shoes or shirt.

I think, *'Okay wings, open,'* and they do. My mind is controlling my wings.

I'm outside my house and begin running down the street for take-off, and I do! Up, up and away!

It's a joyful feeling flying over the top of houses, over the sea, a slight detour and I'm flying over farmland. The cows in the paddock all look up at me as I give them a wave.

'Wow, this is awesome. Look at me everyone, I'm an angel!'

Oddly, there isn't a soul around.

This is one of those dreams that I never want to wake up from. I enjoy this feeling of being a free spirit and able to go anywhere that I please.

Whack!

I feel a smack to the back of my head. Still airborne, I can't help but notice that day has become night; the moonlight and stars barely light up the landscape underneath me. In front of me, radiantly glowing in the moonlight, I see big black shining wings lightly flapping in the slight breeze of the cool autumn night. Attached to the wings is a muscular male body, he's only wearing tight black pants, I can't see his face.

Smack!

I receive another hard hit to the back of my head.

'Ouch! How does he reach behind me like that?'

In retaliation, not knowing my own strength, I whack him back really hard with one of my wings and send him flying backwards.

He regains his composure and darts back towards me through the cool night air. He outstretches his legs and he kicks me hard in the chest, knocking me tumbling backwards in mid-air.

My adrenaline kicks in. I've never felt so strong and fearless. With my new-found strength, I'm able to quickly regain my composure and fly up extremely fast above him. I have him in my sights and fly directly towards him, my arms outstretched and hands raised up. I push him in the chest as hard as I can. I watch as he goes tumbling and spiralling out of control. Feathers fall off his wings as he plummets, landing hard on the grassy paddock below us.

I feel a mixture of rage and adrenaline pulsating through every vein in my body; immediately diving steadily and swiftly down after him. I notice the cows that were previously milling in the paddock are now all cowering under a group of trees.

I land in front of this black angel as he stands up to face me, his wings retracted, chest forward, shoulders back in a show of masculinity and strength. His glowing red eyes focus on mine; the moonlight shines down on him like a spotlight, it was then I see his face.

Jacob!

DAVID GOLDON

Chapter Eleven:
Miss Duffy

I was leaving on my way for a run when I noticed Gabriella attracting my attention by waving her arms in the air in a theatrical manner.

"Michael, Michael," she called, "I'm going to give you a psychic reading seeing as the angel cards didn't work too well last time, come by my house at six tonight."

I agreed and set off on my run.

Reaching the end of my street, I decided to run to the football oval, not far from the beach, and do a bit of a workout on the outdoor exercise equipment there.

It was a wonderful day, sunny, not too hot and a slight cool breeze. I ran past houses, shops and small parks with playground equipment.

I find running quite therapeutic, it gives me time out to think or to not think. I just love the freedom of it. The only sound I hear is my feet as they hit the pavement, *tap tap*, *tap tap* and then my breath, *psssst*. *Tap tap*, *tap tap*, *psssst*; a mechanical rhythm like a machine perfectly in time. My legs power through in perfect synchronisation. I feel like a machine, a running machine.

Jacob weighed heavily on my mind as I ran. Those amazingly beautiful yet dangerous looking eyes, pale face and rosy cheeks. How I admired his courage and arrogant confidence. His constant perusal of me. The warnings the neighbours had given me to stay away from him.

Beeeeeep! Screech!

I stood frozen in the middle of the road; a car stopped incredibly close beside me, the noise of the horn pulsating through me. I turned and looked at the driver. He was furious and yelled out, "Watch where you're going, you fucking idiot!"

In shock, I walked straight ahead and off the road. Dazed, I headed over to a tree and sat down on the ground beside it. The car drove off. My heart was racing; I was shaking and gasping for air while I tried to take in what had just happened. My head was pounding.

'I wasn't hit by the car, but I could have been. Michael, you idiot, don't lose focus, you could have just died.'

I felt a slight déjà vu sensation.

I regained my composure, settled my nerves, stood up and steadied myself against the tree. Looking down at the trunk of the tree I laughed to myself thinking, *'Michael, your legs are like tree trunks,'* and continued running to the oval.

* * *

Still shaken by what had happened on my run, I dropped by Gabriella's place at 6pm as requested.

"You like helping people Michael. You are kind and loving to all living beings. You give them strength and encouragement, and they feel better after they have been touched by your presence. I can feel that you accept and complete challenges that are set for you. You resist temptations, and you help others without reward or praise. The goodness inside you is pure, and you aim to spread your love and kindness to others."

'Wow! Me, really?'

Gabriella continued, "There is a bright, bright light shining within and all around you Michael."

She said in a more serious tone, "Bathe in the goodness of the light. Head for the light. It will allow you to go gently to your chosen path. The healthy, happy light. Don't be afraid."

'What's she talking about, I'm not dead. She must have eaten one too many of those special cookies.'

Then she snapped out of her trance-like state. "Well, champagne darling?"

"I could do with a whole bottle right about now!'

"Yes, please my dear, I want to hear that cork pop!" I say to her in my campest manner.

"Here you go darling, cheers!" she announces as she hands me a flute full of bubbles. "So, how was the reading, any revelations or messages that resonate with you dear?"

"Well, nothing that I didn't already know, like... I am an awesome guy, for example."

"Michael don't be so flippant, the spirits have used me as their vessel, you must listen to what they say, and they will set you on the right path to enlightenment."

"You know I'm not really into all that spiritual stuff, don't you, Gabriella?" I responded rather dismissively.

"Oh, my little lamb, you are destined for something better than this life you have created for yourself. Open your eyes and your mind my darling; the world isn't so black and white." Gabriella sounded slightly annoyed with me.

"I love my life, this town, my wonderful neighbours; even the weather is lovely and sunny every day. I don't have any problems, except Jacob."

'Hmmm... the weather... every day?'

"Darling, you do have a lovely life here, and I'm so glad to be in it, but you'll have to leave sometime, right?"

"No Gabriella, happy to stay in this town and even probably retire here. Unless you want to get rid of me?" I laugh. "But right now, I gotta get ready and head off to work. Later dear."

* * *

Not long into my shift, I called by Miss Duffy's room.

Angela Duffy is a dear lady; I have a lot of time for her. When it's quiet on the ward, I will often have a chat with her. Miss Duffy has a sister who lives interstate but is too old and frail to visit, which is a shame, as she has no other family. She was never married and has no children.

She shares her ward with three other beds, all empty at the moment. A hospital room is quite a depressing environment to spend your last days in so often I'll buy some flowers for her to brighten up the room. The warm smile she gives me in return makes it all worthwhile.

"Oh, Nurse Michael, would you be so kind as to pour me a glass of water? You know in my frail condition that water jug is just too heavy for me to lift."

"No worries Miss Duffy," I said cheerfully as I filled up her glass with some water. "There you go. How are you feeling today?"

"Nurse Michael, you know I am not long for this world. Well, I did have my 80th birthday not long ago, so I made it this far. The one regret I have is that I never married or had children. I guess I just couldn't find the right man or he couldn't find me," she chuckled. "Who would have thought that as I lay on my death bed, I meet the most perfect man ever? Oh, Nurse Michael, he is so handsome, smart and really funny. We laugh a lot, he has made me so happy and, dare I say it..."

Miss Duffy beckoned me closer and whispered in my ear, "He has even proposed to me and, of course, I have accepted! Now I will have no regrets when I finally pass."

"Wow, um... congrats, that's great Miss Duffy, tell me more." I was a little surprised.

"Well, I was here in my bed reading the newspaper, and he came up and asked me if there was anything I needed. When I looked up from the newspaper, I noticed his kindly baby blue eyes and how he looked at me so lovingly, so caring. He smiled such a sweet smile; he has movie star looks, lots of beautiful silver hair parted to the side and beautiful wrinkles in all the right places. I thought I must have dozed off and dreamt him up, but no, he stood there just like you are now.

"He asked what my biggest regret was, and I said, 'It's that I never married.' He said he would be honoured to grant me his hand in marriage as my dying wish. He proposed to me as I lie here on my death bed. I was so overcome by his kindness and generosity so, of course, I accepted. He knows I don't have much money and he said he wasn't interested in what little assets I have. All he said he wanted was to be my soul mate, all he wanted was my soul. Such a sweet, loving, kind man. So I said, 'Yes my darling, you can have my soul. We will be soul mates. I love you.' After that, he said he was so looking forward to making me his and that he will be back for me soon. I just hope I don't die before he comes back."

"Miss Duffy, that sounds so romantic, he will give you a reason to hold on to life as long as you can, to enjoy the happiness that has eluded you for so long. I am so very happy for you."

I shed a little tear of joy for Miss Duffy. She is such a lovely woman. Patients like her make my job a joy, but I try not to get too close to the palliative patients as the pain when they pass really upsets me.

"Sounds like a dreamboat, Miss Duffy. I look forward to meeting him."

"Oh dear, you already know him, he works here as an orderly. His name is Jacob."

I started laughing inside; *'The silly old dear has obviously confused the names.'*

"Here's your meds Miss Duffy, be sure to take them," I said smiling and continued along with my duties.

Chapter Twelve:
Beach

As I lay in bed thinking about the new day unfolding, about Jacob and what my next move would be, I heard light footsteps heading up the stairs to the front door. Having a bedroom at the front of the house means I usually hear everything that's going on outside on my street. The footsteps then retreated away from the front door.

I got out of bed and made my way to the window. Ever so carefully I lifted a slat of the wooden Venetian blind just a little and looked out into the front yard. I couldn't see anyone outside. I walked to the front door and slowly opened it to see a blood red rose and a small card on my doormat. I reached over and picked them up.

The card read: "*Meet me at the beach - 1pm today – Jacob.*"

I still felt guilty over the way he stormed out of my house the other night after I had a little meltdown just as things were getting steamy between us. I guessed he was giving me a second chance.

'*Oh, hang on, it was him pursuing me,*' I remembered, '*I guess I did give in to temptation just a little; well just a taste and no harm done. Why is it I keep resisting his charms and constant sexual advances?*'

I still couldn't quite determine why I wouldn't allow myself to succumb to his charms. I sensed there was something dark and dangerous about him and if I give into his darkness, I could be in some kind of serious danger.

'I do love to flirt with danger,' I admitted to myself, *'I find it sexy and exciting. Perhaps that's why I continue to see him.'*

'No, hang on, it's him who keeps seeking me out,' I realised. *'Well, at least with this invitation to the beach, I get a choice. The day looks to be another fine warm and sunny one, so yes, sexy Jacob, I will accept your invitation. Now, what to wear?'*

* * *

I drove down to the beach to the same location where we met last time. I gathered this was where we were supposed to meet. It was 1.03pm; I couldn't see him, so I sat on the bench seat overlooking the wide expanse of sand and watched the waves in the distance as I waited. Being a weekday, no one else was around so he should be easy enough to spot.

In the distance, I saw something shining brightly. It was coming from the sand dunes, which intrigued me. I looked around, still no sign of Jacob. I took off my flip-flops and walked over the soft, warm sand that slightly squeaked beneath my feet as I headed towards the shiny object.

As I closed in on the bright, curious object that shone like a diamond in the sand, a head wearing a cap and sunglasses popped up and yelled out, "Over here mate!"

'Oh, there he is, but what's that shining object with him?'

Closing in on Jacob I focused on the now blinding light in front of me. Eventually, I was able to see it; a silver champagne tub full of ice and a bottle of champagne!

"What's all this then?" I asked Jacob.

He stood up wearing only black swimming briefs. He took a few steps towards me and greeted me with a kiss on the lips and a hug. "Come over here; I have a surprise for you."

As I approached, I saw a large blanket on the sand and all types of yummy goodness on display; gourmet cheeses, strawberries and, of course, the champagne.

"Wow Jacob, you really have gone all out. I'm confused as well as impressed."

"Well..." Jacob started, "I guess you are the kind of guy that responds to romance, not the overt sexual come-ons that I've tried. I really, really like you Michael, and want to have you in my life as more than just a friend."

I intentionally didn't respond to him. I fell silent for a while trying to process what was happening; I hadn't expected anything like this.

"Wow, all my favourite things. How did you know?" I eventually responded.

"Sit, sit," he motioned me to the picnic rug.

I sat down as he handed me a glass of bubbles and a plate of the gorgeous nibbles he had prepared. We engaged in small talk while we ate and drank.

"Let's go for a dip!" Jacob said quite excitedly.

I peeled off my t-shirt and shorts. Luckily, I had swimming briefs on underneath, and we ran off to the edge of the water.

I stood in the sea at ankle height, "It's too cold!" I yelled.

Jacob came up behind me.

"Don't be a pussy," he laughed. Then he picked me up with his strong arms, took a few steps into the water and dropped me in it.

We walked out a bit further; the water didn't feel as cold now. We jumped up in the air with each coming wave. Jacob grabbed my arm and pulled me in close to him as he kissed me deeply; all I could taste was salt as I felt his tongue swirling around in my mouth...

Everything is dark; I can't breathe, I feel pressure on my head.

Silence.

I hear faint music.

I break the surface of the water gasping for air, coughing and spitting salty water out of my mouth.

"What the hell!" I yelled as I violently broke free of Jacob's grip and swiftly made my way out of the water to the shore. I sat on the water's edge, waves gently lapping at my feet. I continued to cough and spit water out of my mouth.

Jacob strode out of the water quickly and knelt down next to me. "Are you alright?" he said in a most concerned voice.

"You tried to fucking drown me. How do you think I feel?"

Jacob attempted to comfort me by putting his arm around me but I pushed it away. "Fucking murderer. Keep away from me!"

My emotions were all over the place. I begin to sob uncontrollably.

"Michael, what are you talking about? I just saved your life, you had one of your blackouts, and I pulled you up out of the water."

"You did?" I always see the best in people, so Jacobs's response made sense.

'*Lately, it seems I often suffer from blackouts,*' I began to realise.

The first time I had a blackout was when I first met Jacob. It was outside my house; I embarrassingly had one right in front of him. I thought it was just because I couldn't believe how good looking he was; the man of my dreams. Since then though, I'd had a few others in front of some of my neighbours, luckily, they were there to look after me.

"I'd never hurt you Michael. I'm falling in love with you," Jacob said while gently brushing the wet hair off my face.

I allowed him to gently engulf me with his muscular arms while we sat on the water's edge. The feeling of being in his arms felt comforting, safe. I began to get my emotions under control and realised that he just said he was falling in love with me!

I began to sob again. My head was spinning, all these emotions confused me. I couldn't make sense of what had just unfolded.

'*Focus Michael, calm down and breathe, that's it, calm, calm.*'

I fought to get my emotions back in order.

Covered in sand, we both stood up. Jacob took my hand and led me back into the water to wash the sand off, then we returned to our spot on the beach.

"I didn't bring a towel with me Jacob; I didn't know we were going into the water."

"No worries Mikey, I've taken care of that."

'*Mikey, he called me Mikey again.* '

I was still racking my brain trying to think of who used to call me that but no matter how hard I tried it was like the answer had been erased.

'*Oh well, doesn't matter.*'

"Does that mean I'm going to have to call you Jakey?" I asked cheekily.

"You can if you want, Mikey."

"No, actually, I don't. I like the name 'Jacob' better," I responded.

Jacob rubbed his lightly whiskered cheek into mine and we kissed. From that moment I began to feel something for Jacob, I had a new understanding for him; I saw his gentle and caring side. He cared for me and I felt it. I really felt it for the first time. I had no reason to doubt that now.

After we towel dried ourselves Jacob handed me a container of coconut oil sunscreen, "Would you mind oiling me up?" He grinned at me.

I put some oil in my hand and began rubbing it into his chest, it was so firm and muscular. I moved down to his flat stomach with a hint of abdominal muscles beginning to show. I was tempted to move my hand down into his bathing briefs but stopped just at the top of them. I couldn't help but notice the growing size of the organ within.

I got down on my knees and put some more coconut oil in my hand and began to rub the oil up and down his strong muscular legs. Right in my line of sight was that quite impressive package.

"Is that a pistol in your bathers?" I asked playfully.

"Yes, and it's fully loaded and ready to shoot on command," he laughed. "Your turn," Jacob said as he reached down for the container of coconut oil.

I felt his large masculine hands rubbing the oil over my chest.

'The very hands that just saved my life. Or did they?'

His hands made their way down my stomach, and I couldn't even try and stop the excitement growing in my bathers. I felt the abundant amount of sexual tension in the air; I was having slight heart palpitations and shortness of breath.

I jumped a little as Jacob's hand reached into my bathers and held my girth. His hand then slowly retreated as he got down on his knees and rubbed the oil up and down my legs lingering around my crotch area.

"Lie down," he commanded. I submitted to his strong, powerful voice. I felt like the master had spoken and I must obey. I laid down on my stomach.

Jacob straddled me and poured some oil on my back. Rubbing it in circles over my shoulders gently and deeply massaging my still sore shoulder blades, he carried out the task much more sensually than Viktor, my massage therapist would do. He worked my shoulder blades quite deeply with his fingers and thumbs, transfixed on that particular area.

"Ouch, that hurts," I squealed as I felt something pop.

"Sorry. How are you feeling?"

"Amazing! You are certainly experienced at this." I replied in a totally relaxed manner almost slurring my words.

I felt like I was floating on clouds. Especially after my horrific recent near-death experience in the ocean. But I was saved by my hero who was now transporting me into another realm with his magic hands.

His hands moved down to my lower back, suddenly he pulled my bathers down exposing my lily-white butt to the world. He poured some more oil on my lower back allowing it to trickle down in between my butt cheeks. He firmly kneaded my butt cheeks one at a time.

I was in a state of ecstasy. I knew where this was heading.

'Will I let him go there or not? The beach has been deserted since we've been here, and he did save my life. My new-found affection for him has forced me to let down my guard.'

'What about all those warnings my neighbours gave me about him? They never did go into details and Jacob is a lovely guy, he obviously cares for me, I can feel it. Those feelings I had about something not being quite right about him seem to have diminished today. I must've been wrong.'

'Oh Michael, you always over think things!'

I snapped my mind back into focus as I felt Jacob's manhood still encased in the light nylon of his bathing suit rubbing up and down against my butt.

'Oh shit, this is it; he's going to do me right here and now!

I was in such a state of euphoria that I decided I would grant permission for him to pound me into submission. I was his for the taking...

"Hei der du sexy gutter! Or as you say in English, hey there you sexy boys!" A loud voice from afar interrupted Jacob's impending possession of me.

I looked up over the sand dune and saw Viktor heading our way as Jacob moved off me. As he walked closer to us, he stopped and stood completely still realising he had interrupted us and looked away. "So sorry boys, don't mind me, I'm from Norway you know, very liberated, no inhibitions, you can just carry on and I will walk away now."

Moment ruined.

"It's all good, Viktor," I said as I pulled up my bathers. Viktor took the extra few steps to reach our little spot on the beach.

"Boys, nice to see you," Viktor said in that gorgeous accent.

"You too Viktor. I must book another appointment with you soon, my shoulders have been hurting a bit lately, you do such a good job of relieving the pain. So does Jacob actually, he just gave me a nice rub down. Oh, have you two met?"

"Yes," said Viktor.

"No," said Jacob.

"Huh?" I was confused.

'Do they or don't they know each other?'

Out of the corner of my eye, I noticed Jacob give Viktor a death stare, a stare that chilled me to the bone. It was like another person was inside Jacob; someone evil.

"What brings you to this very sand dune Viktor? Surely you can't see us from all the way over there on the foreshore?" I asked to break the tension.

"I was at the park on the foreshore doing my usual yoga routine when I spotted something bright and blindingly shiny," he responded cheerily, "I just had to check it out, and here I find you two ummm... getting to know each other."

Jacob picked up a towel and threw it over the champagne bucket. I looked at the dried up remains of our gourmet goodies and the empty champagne bottle.

"I'd ask you to join us Viktor, but there's nothing left, sorry," I said regretfully.

"That's alright Michael, I'm drawn to all things bright and shining, so I just had to make my way over here to investigate. Hope to see you again soon, bye bye."

Viktor walked off into the distance back towards the park.

"I'm getting a bit sunburnt, Jacob. Let's head back," I said as I rolled up the towels.

Chapter Thirteen: Cake

I'd been summoned over to Muriel's house to give her a hand with a few odd jobs. Fluffy greeted me in the usual way by jumping all over me as I made my way to her front door.

"Yoo-hoo, only me!" I yelled out as I walked into her house.

"I'm in the kitchen darling, come on in!" she yelled back at me.

"Coffee my sweet?"

"Yes please," I replied enthusiastically, "I'm feeling a bit tired this afternoon and a gorgeous plunger coffee will hit the spot perfectly. Do you have any cake?"

"Oh Michael, you eat cake? With that body, you don't want to end up with a spare tyre. But then again, I do have plenty of work for you today so you can work it off." She giggled as she handed me my coffee.

As Muriel headed back to the kitchen, she asked, "So, what's all the goss, how're things at work, have you seen Jacob around lately? I'm sure he will be after you, that hideous creature."

"Slow down Muriel, so many questions," I said as I sipped on my coffee. "Work is fine, oh and to answer the second part of your question, Jacob has started working at the hospital as an orderly."

She looked horrified as she returned with cake in hand.

DAVID GOLDON

I was not sure why but continued anyway. "It was a surprise to me; I bumped into him in the locker room. Seems everywhere I go he's turning up; I guess that's what happens in a small town unless he's a stalker? Is that why you warned me off him?"

"Here, have some Angel Fool cake dear, I made it myself," Muriel giggled as if to change the subject.

"Oh, it looks nice Muriel, except I think it's called Angel *Food* cake and what's this fingernail doing in it? Sorry, but I think I'll pass on the cake."

After I quickly finished my coffee, I went outside to start the yard work Muriel had assigned me. Always happy to help her out, I started up the lawn mower and proceeded up and down and side to side mowing the grass. There wasn't much to do, but then I stopped mid-mow.

As I stood there, an odd thought came into my head.

'Who mows my small patch of lawn out the back and front of my house? I don't own a lawnmower and I've never seen or heard anyone else do it.'

The thought kept swirling around in my mind; I was becoming confused. I felt a tap on my shoulder and nearly jumped out of my skin.

"Michael, the lawn looks great, can you be an angel and rake up the leaves now, thank you."

She realised she'd scared me and quickly apologised.

"No, that's fine, I was off in my head somewhere. Sure, I can do the leaves. Will Fluffy be helping me as usual?"

Muriel gave a knowing chuckle as she handed me the rake, the cue for Fluffy to run up and start growling and nipping at it playfully.

"Good boy Fluffy. You help Uncle Michael rake up all those pesky Autumn leaves that keep falling on your lovely grass."

With that, she wheeled the mower away and left us to it.

DAVID GOLDON

Chapter Fourteen: Viktor

"Viktor, your face! What happened to you?" I said in a shocked voice as he opened his front door.

"I'm alright. Just umm, ran into a door. That's why I couldn't see you for your appointment today at the hospital; I can't go to work looking like this."

I didn't know Viktor lived next door to me with Ralph; I don't think we ever mentioned to each other where we lived. Viktor has a room at the hospital where he sees patients and staff requiring massage therapy.

"Come on in, Michael. I had no idea you lived next door. I have a massage table and equipment set up here; I do see some patients here at home after hospital hours."

I noticed Viktor had a slight limp as he escorted me directly into his massage room. The room smelled like hospital disinfectant.

"What's that smell, Viktor?"

"Oh, I'll put on some lovely essential oils for you."

I looked closely at Viktor's face. "Victor, there's quite a few superficial wounds there but nothing that requires stitches. I guess you've already seen a doctor?"

"No, I haven't, but I'll be alright, and you've just had a look. Right, nurse Michael? Now I know you live next door I can pop over if I need to."

I disrobed and lay down on the massage table. Viktor placed a towel over me, it also smelt like disinfectant.

"So Michael, I guess it's the same spot that's troubling you, shoulder blades?"

"Yes, it is, the pain doesn't seem to ease much. After you've weaved your magic hands over me I get some relief; then the pain returns a few days later."

"I'll try something new with you today; it's called cupping. I just place these small glass cups over your back and light them; they assist in sucking out all the toxins and may help alleviate the pain in your shoulder blades. It may hurt a little bit. Okay, here we go."

As Viktor placed the cups on my back, they did hurt a little, but hey, I'm tough.

"So, Viktor, tell me the truth about those marks and bruises on your face and I couldn't help but notice your limp."

"Like I said Michael, I walked into a door and then tripped over."

"Viktor, I'm a nurse, and your injuries are not consistent with what you say happened."

While the cups were sucking away slightly painfully on my back, Viktor began massaging my legs without replying to my question.

I wondered if Ralph was assaulting Viktor. I didn't know him all that well but I doubted he would be capable.

'I don't know what their relationship is. I didn't even know they lived together until Viktor contacted me to change the location of today's appointment. So the assault must have happened last night. I didn't hear any disturbances coming from Ralph's house last night; I'm a

deep sleeper so it's possible I wouldn't have heard anything. Poor Viktor, he is such a lovely and caring person; whoever did this to him, well, I just can't imagine who.'

My mind was running rampant with thoughts about who could possibly assault Viktor and why.

Obviously, Viktor didn't want to talk to me about it, I should've let it go, but I couldn't. It hurt me deeply that someone could hurt another person in such a vicious and cruel way. I decided I'd have to keep an eye on Viktor in the future.

"So, how's your man, Michael?" Viktor asked deflecting my question.

"He's not my man, but things seem to be headed that way," I responded as best I could with my head in the hole of the massage table. "We are just taking it slowly. I didn't care for him much at first, apart from his devilish good looks, but looks aren't everything, right? He has been teasing me since the day we met by being sexually overt, but that didn't work. The last time I saw him was when he set up a romantic picnic at the beach a few days ago, the day he saved me from drowning. That was the day that you discovered us in the dunes."

'Oh, hang on, when I introduced them Viktor said he had met Jacob previously and Jacob denied knowing Viktor. Then that death stare! It's all coming back to me now; Jacob gave Viktor the darkest, the evilest look I have ever seen. No, it can't be; could Jacob have viciously hurt my cute innocent Viktor?'

As usual, my mind began spinning out of control.

'Does Viktor have some dirt on Jacob, maybe they were dating, or Jacob and Viktor have been together, and

I'm not to find out about them? Everyone keeps telling me to keep away from him. I'll have to do some discreet investigative work on this.'

"So, Viktor, how do you know Ralph?" I asked in my best discreet detective voice.

"I was looking for somewhere to live after I moved into town and answered an advertisement Ralph placed looking for a housemate. It was shortly after that I began working at St Angelina's hospital as a massage therapist."

"How do you and Ralph get along?"

"Oh, very well, just like brothers. He's such a lovely guy and no Michael, he wasn't the one who bashed me."

"A-ha!" I yelled as best I could with my face still lodged in the massage table, "So you do admit someone assaulted you and you didn't walk into a door!"

"You got me!" Viktor replied in that cute accent.

"So who was it, who did this to you? They'll have me to answer to," I demanded to know as I rose up from the massage table. "Ouch, that hurts!" I squealed as some of the cups fell off my back.

Viktor gently pushed me back into lying position again. "Relax Michael, it's going to be alright, I am just going to take these cups off your back now." I heard the cups pop as they came off my back and it kind of hurt too.

Viktor moved to the front of the massage table and gently rubbed the temples on the side of my head. "Relax, Michael, relax..."

I drift off to sleep. I can faintly hear angelic voices, they're singing. I can just barely hear the words *"having the time of your life"*. The singing voices give me such a joyous, uplifting feeling, it feels like they are calling me to join with them. I feel wonderful, I'm floating and carefree listening to the angels sing. Suddenly I start plummeting downwards; everything goes dark, I fall softly to the ground.

'Where am I?'

I have no idea.

The darkness is everywhere; I can only hear my breath. I stand up and look into the darkness. Soon after there's a slight light poking through some clouds that weren't there before. I hear a swooshing noise coming from above me. I look up and see a white angel flying up into the sky, he's wearing white pants, no shirt or shoes. I get a quick glimpse of his face as he swoops high into the sky. It's Viktor!

I'm now surrounded by a white mist but nothing else.

'Oh, shit, I'm dead, aren't I?'

Just then a black angel flies out of nowhere and begins attacking the white angel. They whack each other with their wings. Suddenly I remember that I had a dream like this not long ago. The black angel was Jacob, he was attacking me. I scream out but have no voice.

"Michael, Michael!" I hear someone calling my name; they're shaking me...

"That was some dream you were having there," Viktor said. "Guess I made you a little bit too relaxed," he giggled.

DAVID GOLDON

Chapter Fifteen: Liar

"Yes, Mr Burgess. No, Mr Burgess..." It was another one of *those* nights attending to Mr Angelo Burgess.

He becomes particularly cantankerous in the evening when I'm the only nurse on duty. I sometimes wonder if the old coot tries to wind me up on purpose.

I finally got him settled and gave him a sedative to help him sleep.

"Jacquie!" he said.

"Jacob!" I said at the same time.

"Huh, what?" we said together.

Jacob had entered the room and as soon as he saw me, he turned and left in a mighty hurry.

"Did you see her? That was Jacquie, the female orderly I was asking you about. The one that was going to help me with that IT deal I was telling you about. You must have scared her off, you fool. One look at you and she was out the door. See, nothing wrong with me," Angelo said, slurring his words as the sedative took effect and he drifted off to sleep.

'*What the hell just happened? That was definitely Jacob I saw come into the room just now and vanish like a flash once he saw me. Why is Angelo so sure it was this female orderly named Jacquie he has recently been asking me about? Jacob, Jacquie the names are similar. Maybe Jacob cross-dresses and gives Angelo a lap dance for money? The old guy is loaded, after all.*'

I chuckled to myself then stepped outside of Angelo's room and made my way down the corridor, keeping my eyes peeled for Jacob. It was rare for an orderly to come up to the wards in the evening.

'It's definitely Jacob I saw; it must have been the sedative kicking in that distorted Angelo's vision when he thought he saw his so-called Jacquie.'

I continued with my rounds.

* * *

I was under Miss Duffy's bed reaching out for something that she'd dropped which rolled under there. I saw the legs of someone approaching her bed. I could tell by the uniform pants it was an orderly, obviously Jacob. I wondered what he would be doing approaching Miss Duffy, so I stayed under the bed, unbeknown to Jacob, to suss out the situation.

"Hello my sweetheart, how are you today?" Jacob asked.

"So excited to be seeing you again my gorgeous husband to be," Miss Duffy cooed. "Michael, Michael, where are you? Jacob is here."

I rose up from under Miss Duffy's bed and placed the item I retrieved on her bedside drawers. I looked at the figure that was standing on the other side of the bed holding Miss Duffy's hand. My vision was slightly blurred, I couldn't quite make out his face, and then it came into focus. Jacob. My Jacob though, not the older-gentleman-Jacob that Miss Duffy had previously described. He looked at me with a confused and intrigued expression on his face.

"Ummmm, Jacob, what's going on?" I asked him.

Cautiously he replied, "Eerrrr, I'm just visiting Angela here."

"Michael, you must be at our wedding. Of course, it will have to be here in the hospital. I hope at least I can get out of this bed on our special day, though we haven't decided the date just yet," Miss Duffy said as she lovingly looked at Jacob while stroking his hand.

"Are you sure this is what you want, Miss Duffy?"

"Yes, Michael, it is!" she snapped at me. "All I have ever wanted is to be married and now, for the first time in my life, someone wants to marry me. It's my dying wish. Michael, I thought you understood."

Even though Jacob was still standing there just across the bed from me, I was becoming quite upset at Jacob's deception. I couldn't hold back any further.

"What's his motivation to marry you, Miss Duffy? Sorry to say but what would be the benefit to Jacob for marrying you? I know you said you don't have much money but why would a fit, healthy, young man like Jacob marry a... more mature lady like yourself. As you know, unfortunately, you are not long for this world and... your husband to be is in love with me!"

She began laughing hysterically. "Michael, have you been raiding the drugs cabinet? Oh, that's so funny. For a moment there I thought I was going to have a heart attack, but not before I get married! As I have told you previously, he's not interested in what little assets I have, all he said he wanted was to be my soul mate, all he wanted was my soul. Isn't that right dear?" she asked turning to Jacob.

He just stood there and smirked.

'The little fucker. I just want to knock that smirk right off his gorgeous face.'

I looked at her quizzically.

She continued, "Michael, look at Jacob, he's way too old for you, sorry dear," she said turning briefly to Jacob, "but you did give me the best laugh I have had in ages."

I stormed out of the room.

Feeling enraged, I waited at the nurse's station ready to pounce on Jacob as soon as he walked past.

'Hang on, what did Miss Duffy mean by "Jacob was too old for me" and why did she find it so highly amusing?'

"Hold it right there mate!" I said to Jacob in the scariest voice I could muster as I pushed him up against the wall. "What the hell are you playing at offering to marry an elderly patient that doesn't have much more time to live?"

He didn't answer, so I shoved him against the wall again, pinning him to it with my forearm resting against his chest.

"Huh? Huh?" I kept repeating as I kept pushing him back against the wall. He looked me right in the eyes while adrenalin was pumping furiously throughout my body.

He smirked and said, "You gonna hit me Mikey? Come on; no one's around. Hit me Mikey. Now's the time. Or you wanna kiss me? Yeah, kiss me Mikey. I know you want to."

He smelt so good, and he was right; I didn't know if I wanted to hit him or kiss him, so I released my grip on him.

He grabbed my waist and pulled me close to him. "You are so hot when you're angry, Mikey. You're turning me on like you wouldn't believe."

'*Oh, I can believe it,*' I thought as I felt him pressing his growing manhood against me.

He put his hand on the back of my head and pushed my face to his and began kissing me. I started to kiss him back; thoughts were swirling around in my head. I pushed him away.

He began to walk away, turned and gave me that irresistible smirk of his.

DAVID GOLDON

Chapter Sixteen: Passing

I arrived at work not looking forward to my double shift that would finish at midnight. Going to my usual ward, I checked the patient list.

'Another quiet day ahead by the look of it.'

I walked toward the room of my favourite patient, Angela Duffy, to say hi and see how she was doing. I got to her bed and it was empty. I guessed another nurse had taken her somewhere for some tests or the like.

"Michael, there you are, I've been looking for you," said a slightly out of breath Viktor. "Can you follow me to the nurses' station please?"

We arrived at the nurses' station.

"Michael, the other nurses asked me to speak to you directly because they know we're friends. Unfortunately, Angela Duffy died last night."

I stood there in shock, taking in the words that just left Viktor's lips.

'I shouldn't be feeling like this; I'm a nurse, a professional that deals with this type of thing now and then; I let my guard down and became emotionally attached to a patient.'

"Did she pass away peacefully do you know?" I asked Viktor.

"Well, I heard you grew quite an attachment to her so I would like to say yes, she did pass peacefully. If you're asking me as a professional, I'd have to say no, she didn't. I was here before she was taken down to the morgue, she looked like a shrivelled-up pea; like she had her soul sucked out of her."

"What? I haven't quite heard anyone say anything like that before, what does that mean, her soul sucked out of her?"

"Never mind, Michael, I'll explain later. Right now, it looks like you could do with a hug."

Viktor took me in his arms and held me tight; I hadn't made physical contact with Viktor like this before.

'It feels good, well, amazing actually.'

I felt my pain slowly dissipate from my body. I felt at peace, secure, safe and as one with him.

As Viktor eventually broke his hold of me, he looked me right in the eyes. I felt the strangest sensation. I had the feeling that he knew me, knew all about me, he was so familiar to me, yet not. I had never felt as close to someone as I did right then. I felt a bond, a close bond with him like he had known me all my life.

I came back to my senses and noticed the recent wounds on Viktor's face had completely healed. Viktor realised I was studying his face. His eyes looked deeply into mine.

I swallowed hard as a strange sensation engulfed me. It felt like he had entered my mind; little tentacles extending from his eyes into mine and then wriggling their way into my head. I felt exposed, inside and out. As if he could feel the very essence of me; my whole being was becoming unearthed. He was an intruder into my mind, but an intruder I gave permission to explore me. Any secrets I had he could uncover them.

"I might just hang around here at the nurses' station for a while, Michael. To keep an eye on you, make sure you're alright. I don't have any patients booked in until later."

"I feel much better now Viktor, thanks so much for caring about me; I know you are in your treatment room downstairs if I need you."

"No worries then. I'll be watching over you, see you later."

I watched Viktor as he walked slowly away from me, disappearing into the distance. I felt even closer to him than I had before, as though we shared an intimate bond. Like he was a long-lost friend that had grown up with me and knew everything about me. It felt nice, comforting. I didn't feel lonely anymore, that bond, that feeling. I felt complete.

DAVID GOLDON

Chapter Seventeen: Confused

As the day turned into evening, I felt exhausted as my double shift continued. The hospital ward felt lonely now that Angela Duffy had passed away. Something didn't feel right; I just knew Jacob was involved somehow.

As I walked past Angelo Burgess's room, I could hear muffled voices. I wondered who was in there with him; he didn't usually receive visitors.

My curiosity got the better of me and I stopped in my tracks. I quietly took a few steps back and stood silently outside the door and listened to the conversation, the voices just louder than a whisper.

"So, we have a deal then Angelo, my gorgeous stud muffin?"

"Yeah, yeah, of course. Sounds too good to be true, Jacquie, but I trust you. So let's seal the deal with a kiss then, come over here and pucker up my sweet."

"Oh, Angelo, if only you weren't so infirmed I'd show you a really good time."

"Jacquie, you are too wicked, you evil minx."

"How about I lift up the covers and get your motor running."

I was suddenly in a state of shock. I recognised the voice and before I knew it, I was standing right next to Angelo's bed watching on as someone's head was bobbing up and down under the covers. Angelo lay there with his eyes closed moaning in pleasure.

"What the hell's going on here?" I yelled.

Angelo opened his eyes in shock and shot me a dirty look while the perpetrator's head ceased moving and remained under the covers.

"Piss off you bloody interfering nosey bastard!" Angelo shouted at me.

"Who do we have here?" I said as I pulled the covers off the bed.

"You'll be fired for this, you disgusting, vile creature!" I yelled at Jacob.

Then Angelo yelled at me, "Why don't you just get out of my room. I don't need a nurse, Jacquie is looking after me just fine."

Jacob stood up, took a step towards me, invading my body space and looked me right in the eyes while licking his lips.

"Jacob, I think you'd better leave right now," I warned him.

"Jacquie don't listen to him, you can stay."

Jacob turned and looked at Angelo with that wry smile of his, that smile that I thought was only reserved for me.

"It's fine my stud muffin, I'll leave, but I will be back for my prize real soon," Jacob said coyly and walked out of the room.

"What the hell was that all about nurse man?" Angelo exploded. "You have no right to send her out of my room; I'll have you reported."

"Whoa, hang on Angelo, that was a staff member acting inappropriately with you, and *he* will be reported."

"Yeah, well, nurse man, you better get your eyes checked because that was a woman, that was Jacquie. For some reason you keep denying her existence, well there you go, you just saw her leave the room. I'm not sure if it's the meds or not but were you referring to her as Jacob?"

"Well, yes, that's who it was, Jacob Devlin. He works here as an orderly, I know him quite well."

"Well one of us needs to check into the psychiatric unit or get glasses and it sure isn't me. Do you think I would let a bloke do that to me? Disgusting!"

I picked up the chart at the end of Angelo's bed and examined the medication he was prescribed. There was nothing there that would give him hallucinations except perhaps the small amount of morphine he was on.

Then I recalled the confusion with the recently deceased Miss Duffy.

'She referred to Jacob as an older distinguished man also named Jacob, but he wasn't my Jacob. This is all getting way too confusing.'

"Did this Jacquie woman want anything from you? What was it that he, I mean she, said about returning for a prize?" I asked Angelo inquisitively.

"Just get outta here, I wanna rest now, it's been an exhausting evening."

Later in the shift, as I walked into Mr Burgess's room, I heard a noise... *tap tap, tap tap, psssst*. He had been put on life support; the poor old bugger was not long for this world, I could tell just by looking at him.

Even though he wasn't a particularly nice person, I've always found it sad when a patient passes. I wonder what the future holds for them.

'Is there a future? Are they reincarnated, do they go to heaven, or hell, and do such places even exist. What is it like to be on life support? I hear that you disappear into another world, but you can still hear things going on around you.'

I felt quite sad, deflated and exhausted today as I took Angelo Burgess's hand, "I wish you well on your journey after this life, Angelo."

I propped up his pillow and rearranged the bedding; he looked more comfortable now. I sat next to him while listening to the machine keeping him alive... *tap tap, tap tap, psssst.* Over and over again, a strong, steady rhythm.

I felt I wanted to cry; I wasn't sure why. As I gazed around at the luxurious surrounds of his beautiful hospital suite, I felt a presence. I walked towards the window and noticed what looked to be someone standing behind the curtains which framed the beautiful ocean view. I carefully took hold of the curtain and ripped it open all the way back.

"Oh fuck," I shouted as I felt a hand clamp down hard on my shoulder. I swung quickly around. It was Jacob.

"What the hell man, you frightened the shit out of me!" I yelled at him.

"Hey, quiet mate. A guy is dying over there. A bit of respect." Jacob whispered to me.

I looked at Jacob.

'He is one hell of a beautiful man. So damn sexy and so damn wrong.'

I felt at my lowest ebb; I just wanted to be held, to feel secure, for someone to tell me everything is going to be alright. Just then Jacob wrapped his arms tightly around me; he felt stronger, stronger than before. I didn't resist, I enjoyed the physical contact and began to cry uncontrollably.

'Oh Michael, what a fool. What are you doing? This is the guy who's messing with your head.'

"Just let it all out Mikey, everything is going to be alright," Jacob whispers into my ear. It was just what I need to hear.

'Maybe he isn't so bad after all.'

I think back to Miss Duffy, who Jacob promised to marry before she died.

'She saw an older gentleman named Jacob, while at the same time I saw my handsome, young Jacob.'

My mind drifted off to Angelo imagining Jacob to be Jacquie.

'He was so convinced he was seeing a woman and I only saw Jacob. Am I having difficulty recognising fact from fantasy? Am I losing my mind? Maybe I have been working too much?'

So many bizarre thoughts drifted in and out of my mind.

Jacob sat me down on the overstuffed sofa facing the window and I could see the sunset over the ocean. All the while in the background the *'tap tap, tap tap, psssst'* sound of Angelo's life support continued.

Jacob knelt down in front of me reaching his hand up to my face. He gently placed his thumb on my face and wiped my tears across my cheeks tenderly. I felt I was falling for him all over again. Jacob sat down beside me, reached out and took my hands in his. I turned to him, and he looked into my eyes as I gazed back into his.

"Maybe you need to rest, Mikey. Just lie down here on the sofa, you don't look so well."

"Yeah, I think I just might. Angelo is the only patient in my ward tonight, just for a bit though. Just make sure I'm not here too long though, okay?" I lay down, closed my eyes and let the darkness wash over me.

Suddenly, I sit up and notice night has fallen; the room is dimly lit. I hear the life support machine... *tap tap, tap tap, psssst...* and look over at Angelo's bed. I see a figure leaning over Angelo, their face up close to his. I can't make out who it is at first but then recognise the uniform as belonging to Jacob.

'That's nice of him to be looking out for Angelo while I recover from my exhaustion.'

I can see two small faint red lights that look like they're coming from Jacob's eyes. A bright blue light appears to be coming out of Angelo's mouth going into Jacob's.

Angelo's arms begin to flap about uncontrollably. Jacob leans further over him and pins Angelo's arms down with his hands while the blue light continues to syphon out of Angelo's mouth into Jacob's.

'What should I do, yell out or stay quiet? I don't want to alert Jacob that I'm watching what's happening.'

I feel light headed; my eyes are heavy, they close.

I woke up with a jolt; I sat bolt upright. I heard the life support machine... *beeeeeeeeeee...* Angelo had flatlined. I rushed over to Angelo and noticed his face and arms were shrivelled up like a freeze-dried pea as if he had the life sucked out of him!

Immediately Angela Duffy came to mind. I never saw her after she died but I did recall Viktor saying she looked like she had her soul sucked out of her.

'I couldn't quite understand what he meant then, but I think I do now.'

"Hey, Mikey, I was just coming in to wake you up when I heard the life support machine flatline, has the old guy died?"

"Yes, he has, poor guy, look at the state his body is in, like something from a horror movie."

"Yeah, he does," Jacob replied in an unconcerned manner.

I hadn't seen anything like this before but perhaps Jacob had, judging by the controlled manner of his response. "Mikey, you tidy him up and I'll be right back to take the stiff down to the morgue."

'Jacob can be so insincere.'

DAVID GOLDON

Chapter Eighteen:
Seduced

I woke the next morning with what had transpired the previous night at the hospital going through my head. Jacob either turned into some kind of demonic creature, or I dreamed the whole thing while I slept on the sofa.

"Right, Michael, enough is enough. It's time you confronted all of your neighbours that warned you about Jacob," I said aloud to myself.

As I sat up in my bed, another beautiful, sunny morning welcomed me. I took a moment to listen to the birds chirping outside as I wondered how I would go about confronting Viktor, Ralph, Muriel and Gabriella.

'Have their warnings actually led me to these really bad dreams I'm having about Jacob? What was the reason I've been resisting him for so long after all his subtle and not so subtle advances towards me? Any other time I certainly wouldn't have held back. He's the man of my dreams or my nightmares, I just don't know which.'

'Maybe I should leave this town, I love it here so much, but everything is getting confusing and difficult for me now. I feel like I'm losing my mind, that reality is fading.'

"Focus, Michael. Right, get yourself organised, get out of bed and enjoy your day off," I said out loud.

'Great, now I'm talking to myself!'

I jumped in the shower, the warm water cascading down my body helped calm my mind somewhat; I tried to think of nothing but failed.

After the relaxing shower, I made my way into the kitchen and brewed a lovely cup of coffee; I took it with me into the backyard to enjoy the gentle rays of the morning sun.

'Who will be the first person I confront over their warnings about Jacob,' I wonder. *'I have to do this; I need to get this man out of my head, he's driving me crazy, literally. Viktor and Ralph live within a few feet of me, I can't hear any noise coming from their house. Usually, Ralph is in the garden at this time of the day pottering around.'*

My mind was made up, Viktor and Ralph would be the first I spoke with. I recalled the evil look Jacob gave Viktor that time when I nearly gave myself to Jacob, in the heat of the moment, at the beach. Not to mention that strange vision I had of Jacob assaulting Viktor and them both being angels.

Ding, dong!

I heard the doorbell ring and wondered who the visitor could be.

'I hope it's Viktor.'

I make my way through the house to the front door and open it.

Jacob! There he stood, his perfectly styled black hair, fringe slightly hanging over his forehead looking particularly cute. His eyes were the darkest shade of brown; complementing his rosy cheeks.

He was dressed in what I assumed to be his favourite colour; black. Black tight-fitting polo shirt showing off his muscular frame, accompanied by tight black jeans, same as the first day I had met him.

'Absolutely gorgeous, what's not to like?'

"Are you going to stand there and stare at me all day, Mikey?"

"Oh, yeah, sorry, do you want to come in? I guess that means yes," I say as Jacob walks in right past me.

We made our way through to the backyard and sat where I had been sitting previously.

"I just wanted to check up on you, make sure you are alright. You were acting pretty weird last night at work," Jacob said in a concerned manner.

"Yeah, not bad thanks, just my headspace, think it needs clearing a bit," I explained.

"You wanna talk about it, I'm a good listener. I'm sure I can take away all your pain," Jacob said as he gave me one of his smiles.

'The same smile he gave Angelo before he sucked the life out of him. Focus Michael. Say it, go on and say it.'

"Great day today, huh?"

Jacob nodded.

'Idiot! How can I open the conversation; I need to purge all this nonsense that's piling up in my head, driving me batshit crazy. So, are you a soul-sucking evil angel with red eyes or what? No, too direct, but to the point!'

I began staring at Jacob again; my eyes made their way up and down his biceps, then his chest. They appeared larger, he looked so much stronger than he used to.

"Jacob, can I ask you something?"

"Sure Mikey, whatever you want. Nothing is off limits for you."

"Have you been working out a lot more, your body has really beefed up?"

'Idiot Michael.'

Jacob gave me a cute grin and I melted.

'Michael, there is no way this guy is evil. If you ask him, you know he'll have you committed to the loony bin.'

"So, Jacob, how do you know Viktor, Ralph, Muriel and Gabriella?"

'Good, I said it.'

"Who? I don't," Jacob said quite blankly. "Well, I met that Viktor guy when we were in the sand dunes, Mikey. Remember that? I may have seen him pass by at work. As for the other names; nope, don't know 'em. Why do you ask?"

"They all know you; they told me to keep away from you. Whatever I do, they told me not to have anything to do with you," I spurted out.

'Good one, Michael.'

"So, what do *you* think? Mikey, you like what you see, right?" Jacob said as he flexed his huge biceps and flashed me one of his heart-melting smiles.

"Yeah, well, I kind of think they don't know you like I do. You are, well, totally handsome and we get on really well. I like you a lot and you appear to be the most perfect man I've ever met," I gushed.

"So, the problem is, Mikey?" Jacob smiled.

"Problem is... maybe I shouldn't listen to my nosey neighbours."

"That's right, Mikey. Don't listen to those people that don't even know me. You know me; you know me much better than anyone else. What you see is what you get, or you're going to get."

"Yeah, I suppose you are right," I mumbled.

Jacob got up out of his seat and took my hand. "Come on, let's go inside," he smiled.

He led me into my living room and we sat down close together on the sofa. "You wanna go with me?"

"Go where?" I ask.

"Derr, be boyfriends," he responded cheekily.

"I'll have to think about it," I giggled.

Jacob pushed me down on the sofa, sat on top of me and began caressing my body with his strong masculine hands.

"Just a minute," he said as he got up off the sofa and closed all the blinds blocking out the morning sun.

Jacob took off his polo shirt and boots; I melted more into the sofa at the sight of his perfectly toned body. A body that I was going to be tasting any second.

He re-joined me on the sofa, his hands moving all over my chest. He slid his hands under my t-shirt and gently pulled it over my head and tossed it onto the floor. My hands were now running over his chest.

Voices in my head were telling me to back off; I pushed them aside.

'These silly voices, the voices that almost drove me insane, they aren't real. This is real, just me and my "boyfriend" Jacob, that's real, nothing else matters.'

Jacob began kissing me deeply and passionately, chills ran through my body, jolts of electricity that I had never felt before. I felt like I was being transported into a state of euphoria. It was just the two of us together in that moment.

Jacob whispered something in my ear; I couldn't make out what he was saying.

He said it again, louder this time. "Will you be mine, Mikey, give yourself to me? Let's be soul mates, give your whole self and your soul to me."

He began to nibble at my ear, sending my body into an uncontrollable bout of quivering; I'd never felt such a sensation.

He whispered again into my ear, "Will you be mine, Mikey? Give yourself to me, let's be soul mates, give your whole self and your soul to me."

'*Stop talking,*' I thought.

"Just say yes, Mikey, just say yes."

In the throes of passion, I usually would have said 'yes, yes, yes' but instead, I didn't answer him. Jacob continued saying the same thing; I was getting a bit annoyed.

"Oh will you shut up!" I yelled out at him surprising myself. Jacob drew back a bit in shock at my sudden outburst, then continued to send me into seventh heaven.

"Say yes. Mikey, just say yes," Jacob's sexy voice breathed into my ear. Jacob's voice became louder and more demanding, obsessive even. Instead, I just moaned in pleasure.

"Enough!" I yelled out as I somehow summoned the strength to push this big brute of a man off me. He landed on his back with a thud on the floor. He lay there motionless.

'*Oh shit, he's dead.*'

I straddled him searching for a pulse; I couldn't find one, my heart started to race. I put my cheek next to his mouth and could feel his breath.

'*Phew, he's alive.*'

Jacob's hands suddenly grabbed my throat, holding just tight enough not to choke me. He opened his eyes. Those beautiful dark brown eyes that I gazed into just moments ago had turned a shade of dark red.

Jacob looked angry, really angry. I tried to pull his arms off me but he was too strong. Even though I was in the power position on top of him, I just didn't know what to do.

'The dreams I've been having aren't dreams at all. This red-eyed, evil Jacob is here on the floor with me on top of him. I was right all along; there is something not quite right about him.'

"Say yes, damn you, say yes-you-agree!" Jacob shouted as his grip on my throat tightened.

"No, never!" I yelled as best I could, his powerful hands clutching my throat. "It was you; it was you all along. You killed Angela Duffy and Angelo Burgess."

Jacob gave out the evilest, blood-curdling laugh that sent shivers of fear through my body. His face changed from my gorgeous Jacob to an older man, then to a young woman.

Jacob laughed and laughed as I tried as best I could to release myself from his grip. I slapped him hard in the face and looked on in terror. His eyes became redder, he continued to laugh.

'I'm not a fighter; I don't know how I'm going to get out of this.'

Jacob released his grip on my throat, maneuvered his way out from under me and stood up while I stayed bent over on the floor coughing. "Oh Mikey, you should have just said yes and given me your soul, now, because you didn't, I'm going to have some fun with you until you submit to me."

117

"I'll never submit to you, whatever you are!" I felt a rush of adrenaline pulse through my veins; I jumped to my feet and pushed Jacob hurtling back against the wall behind him.

"I like it when you get rough, Mikey," he laughed as his eyes glowed red. He just stood there, in all his bare-chested glory, taunting me.

'How can someone turn nasty so quickly? Just when I thought I knew him well, just when I was beginning to trust him, just when I was beginning to fall in love with him. I no longer recognise my Jacob, this beautiful bare-chested man that stands in front of me I no longer know. I just see a mean-spirited creature who is trying everything to hurt me. My neighbours were right about him after all.'

He began taunting me. "Mikey, you gonna call your mummy, where's mummy? Oh, mummy, mummy, Mikey needs you, come save your son from evil Jacob!"

'Who is my mother? Where is she?' I started thinking. *'Do I have a mother, of course, I do, don't I? Why can't I remember? Why is Jacob saying this to me?'*

"Nope, no mummy, Mikey? How about your daddy, you going to ask dad to save you from me?"

Jacob got me there as well; I also couldn't recall who my father was.

'What's going on? Why can't I remember?'

Thoughts kept swirling through my mind.

'What's wrong with me? Why can't I remember? Why is Jacob taunting me with this information?'

"Stop, just stop! I don't understand! Why are you saying these things?" I yelled at Jacob.

"It's fun Mikey, it's fun to mess with your mind. You don't even know where you are. I know everything. I know all about you Mikey, more than you know about yourself. By the time I've finished with you, you are going to be begging me to stop. But I won't stop, Mikey; not until you give me your soul."

Jacob was right; he was messing with my head. He had planted seeds in my mind; while I was dealing with his taunting, I was also thinking about what he had said about my parents.

'I'm losing my grip on reality.'

Then, suddenly, he stopped. "Mikey, I'm done with you. You are one tough nut to crack, but I'll be back for you, I like the challenge. You'll just never know who to trust anymore. I could appear at any time in any form, and you won't know it's me, you just won't know."

Jacob disappeared into a mist and vanished!

'My handsome, perfect man, gone, just like that. I'm sure I'm going to wake up and find out this was just another one of those weird Jacob dreams. Maybe I've had another one of my blackouts, oh geesh, I could be laying on a floor somewhere.'

"Snap out of it Michael," I tell myself, "None of this is real."

DAVID GOLDON

Chapter Nineteen: Realisation

I opened my eyes after waking from a deep sleep. It seemed only a minute ago I had drifted off.

My bedroom was cloaked in darkness apart from the rays of moonlight streaming through the timber Venetian blinds, casting lines across the polished timber floorboards. My hands were warm, quite warm and a bit clammy.

I felt a sensation like water trickling down my right hand, but as I wiped it with my left hand, it wasn't actually wet. That was rather odd, so I reached for the bedside lamp and turned it on.

My head began pounding, which I'd been getting used to.

'I hope I don't have another one of my famous blackouts. Actually, maybe I should call for help; these symptoms are worrying me slightly.'

I got out of bed and looked around for my phone; I couldn't find it. The warmth of my hands was still present, and the thumping of my head was increasing. I made my way to the kitchen and turned on the cold-water tap. Running the cold water over my hands had no effect, they still felt oddly clammy.

'This is not normal; I better go and seek help from one of my neighbours.'

I went back into the bedroom and put on a dressing gown, something on my feet and made my way outside.

It was cool out in the street and quite misty; the moon was full and shone down on me like a spotlight, painting the world around me in blue and silver. It felt magical.

I looked around at my neighbours' houses for any sign of light to indicate that someone was still awake at this time of night. I noticed the warm glow of yellow light emanating from Ralph's house; I gathered either he or Viktor must be awake, thankfully the closest house to me.

As I walked the short distance to Ralph's house my hands still felt extremely warm; my head continued pounding. My legs suddenly became like jelly as I wobbled my way into Ralph's front yard. I fell to the ground and crawled along on my hands and knees up the three front steps to the door. I didn't have the strength to knock on the door; my whole body was weak and limp.

I lay there on the veranda underneath the window where the light was coming from. I tried to call out. I just didn't have the strength. I just lay there totally incapacitated. I heard voices coming from inside the house. I heard Ralph and Viktor speaking in quiet voices.

"I think we are just going to have to tell him," I heard Ralph say.

"I think you may be right, but you know the rules; we can't tell him, he has to try and realise for himself."

"I have certainly given him enough clues to try and drag him out of it; he loves it here so much he doesn't want to leave," Gabriella said.

'*Huh? Is Gabriella in there with Ralph and Viktor? That's odd,*' I thought, as their voices became louder in my head.

"He has passed every test I have given him with flying colours; he's definitely earned his place." It was Muriel's voice this time.

'So that's Ralph, Viktor, Gabriella and Muriel in there, how rude of them not to invite me to a neighbourhood soiree. Focus, Michael, try and move, yell anything...' but I couldn't.

There was laughter, a lot of laughter.

'If only they knew I lay out here probably dying and they're all laughing.'

There were lots of light-hearted conversations happening at the same time.

"You sure look pretty."

"Oh, you like?"

"You should dress like that more often."

"Does this colour suit me do you think, who does your makeup dear?"

"We are just having too much fun, no wonder he doesn't want to leave, nor would I," someone else cackled.

"I've just got to take this hideous kaftan off," I heard Gabriella say in her unmistakable deep voice.

"I'm going to take my dress off; thank goodness I didn't wear heels as well," Muriel laughed. I heard a loud swoosh noise. "Ahhh, that feels much better."

Then I heard a few other swoosh noises.

"Shhhh, quiet everyone, I'm sensing him." I heard Viktor say, while I lay unable to move or speak under the window of the room where they were all having a party. A party without me!

I heard the front door open and saw two bare feet step out onto the front door mat. As my eyes made their way up the figure, I saw white linen pants, a slim waist, and a bare muscled chest; I recognised the face in the radiant moonlight.

'*It's Viktor.*'

He took a few steps towards me, bent over, placed one arm under my legs and the other under my neck. Gently he picked me up off the cold wooden floorboards. I noticed something white shining brightly in the moonlight behind his back.

'*Wings?*'

Viktor carried me into a room and laid me on a sofa. "Hey, Raphael, Michael is in a bad way. You are the healer. Can you work a little bit of your magic on him now, please?"

The guy that Viktor called out to quickly made his way over to me in the dimly lit room. I couldn't see his face properly; I did notice he was dressed the same as Viktor, white linen pants and shirtless. He moved his hands up and down my body and immediately I began to feel better. I regained my strength and sat up on the sofa. I felt renewed.

I looked up at this Raphael guy standing in front of me; he also had white wings tucked up behind his back. He had a concerned look on his face, and immediately I recognised him.

'*Ralph! Okay, have I just interrupted some kind of fetish plaything between Ralph and Viktor?*' I think to myself, '*Or am I in one of those adult movies? Maybe I'm just hallucinating?*'

I rose slowly from the sofa to my feet and looked over at Viktor then back to Ralph. "Well, is this a private party or what?" I ask with a giggle. "Sorry guys, whatever you did, Ralph, I feel a lot better. Thank you so much, but I best be making my way home now and leave you two to it."

"Michael, stay right where you are," Viktor said in a harsh, manly, but still sweet sexy accent.

"Oh, Viktor, I haven't heard you speak like that before; so butch. Can I touch your wing?" I ask playfully.

"Michael, we don't have much time. Things are about to change for you. I am here for you to help guide you through what is about to happen, just as I have guided you through so many obstacles since the day you were born."

"Viktor, now you are scaring me, what's going on?" I asked as I trembled a little.

"I will be as gentle as I can but, you know, I need to move fast before time runs out. You see this guy here, Ralph as you refer to him? His name is Raphael; he is an angel. Touch his wings a little bit; you will see they are real."

I reached out my hand and felt the firm white feathers, I stepped behind him and noticed his back was rippling with muscles. I stroked the base of his wings, and they were coming directly out of his shoulder blades, no strings and no tricks that I could make out in the dim light of this room.

"Well, they do actually appear to be real," I said in astonishment.

I walked over to Viktor and ran my hands up and down his wings; I began having flashbacks of the dreams that I'd been having about angels. Oddly, all those dreams were beginning to make sense; I no longer thought they were dreams at all.

"Can you errr ladies come in here please," Viktor called out.

'Oh yes, that's right, Muriel and Gabriella are here. They were talking while I lay outside,' I remembered.

"Michael, now, before I introduce the ummm, ladies, are you feeling alright? You know, not too overwhelmed yet?"

"No, Viktor, I think I'm doing fine so far, thank you."

In through the door walked two other figures, they stood in front of me. One of the figures spoke in a bright, friendly tone, "Hi Michael, it's me," said the unmistakable husky voice of Gabriella.

The room became brighter. Standing before me was a face I vaguely recognised, but it looked different somehow. Then I realised, she had no makeup and Gabriella were a man!

I stood there with my mouth open, nothing to say for once, I couldn't even come up with a wisecrack.

My attention and confusion turned to the other figure that entered the room with Gabriella. As I looked at him he said, "If I knew you were coming I would've baked a cake, an Angel *Fool* cake, of course!" and he erupted into laughter followed by the others. By the comment he made I realised this handsome guy was actually Muriel!

"It's Angel *Food* cake!" I replied cheekily.

Chapter Twenty: Release

The atmosphere in the room was electric; I *knew* these four guys standing in front of me in their angel outfits, I felt an amazing bond with these guys. "I'm a bit confused can someone tell me what is happening?"

"Allow me to start, Michael. My name is Gabriel and I am an angel," he said like he was introducing himself at an AA meeting. "You know me better as Gabriella the great psychic; well that's what you made me," she/he said in a typically theatrical manner.

"Funny one, Gabriel. That leaves me. Michael, my name is Uriel, not Muriel. Congratulations by the way, you passed all of the good deed tests I put you through."

"Okay, so let me get this straight. Your name is really Raphael, not Ralph, you are Gabriel, not Gabriella and you're Uriel, not Muriel. Hang on a tick; they are the Arch Angel names; you're just missing a Michael."

I looked at Viktor and said, "So, Viktor, you must really be Michael?"

"No, that's not me," he smiles.

"You are kidding me; you mean to say that I am Arch Angel Michael?" I pumped my fist up in the air.

"Tickets much?" laughs the handsome Uriel. "No, Michael, you are just his namesake as we all are. We just happen to have the same names as the big boss angels."

I felt a little embarrassed as I turned to Viktor, "So, Viktor, that still leaves you. Where do you fit into all this madness?"

"Michael, I mentioned it to you before but, with all that has just been revealed to you, you have forgotten. My real name *is* Viktor. Yes, I am Norwegian. This is how I looked, how we *all* looked the day our human form died. But enough about us, I must explain some things to you quickly. Actually, come outside with me."

Viktor opened the front door and I walked out onto the veranda. He followed me with Gabriel before me, Raphael behind me and Uriel on my left side. In the darkness, moonlight lit up the trees and garden in Ralph's, I mean Raphael's, front yard.

"Michael, to answer the rest of your question about where I fit into everything that is unfolding right before you now; I was assigned to you the day you were born. I was there with you every time you fell over and scraped your knee, every birthday, Christmas, celebration and so forth. I was there guiding you during your darkest days; I wiped away your tears; I was there when you met your partner, Paul. You know, things do happen for a reason. Sometimes I am providing you with options or opportunities. You choose your path to learn and grow and be wise; I just guide you along on your journey."

"So, you are like my Guardian Angel, is that what you are trying to tell me, Viktor?"

"Yes, that's right Michael, I am."

"Okay, then where am I? This is a dream, right?" I ask.

"Michael," Viktor pauses. "You are dead. Well, almost."

I stood there in silence looking out into the misty blue night, just me surrounded by four angels. Viktor was standing in front of me; he appeared to be shedding a tear.

"Alrighty then," I said in a bright but condescending manner, not believing anything he was telling me. "If you, Viktor, are such a bloody great Guardian Angel, how is it exactly that I'm supposedly almost dead and still living and loving this amazing town?" I ask him with annoyance in my voice.

"Michael, when your time is up, it's up. There's nothing I can do but guide you on your way to whatever destiny is ahead of you."

"So how did I end up here? It all seems real to me. You haven't drugged me have you?"

"No, no, of course not," Viktor laughs. "You were out running; you love to run. Do you remember? You were running across a road when you were hit by a car, your body flew into the air and smashed against a tree. That's why we kept telling you your legs are like tree trunks; to try and help you regain your memories to get you out of this coma your human form is still currently trapped in."

Viktor continued, "This whole town of Engle Byen was created by you, your dream destination. You controlled almost everything that was happening, we just tweaked it a little bit. When you went into the coma I went with you; I can't leave you until you are fully released from your human form, it is then you no longer need me. Because of all the kindness and good deeds you did while human, it was decided by the powers that be that you would be granted the honour of becoming a guardian angel on the passing of your human form. Here in your state of coma, and being destined to become an angel, Jacob got word and entered this realm to try to get you to give your soul to him. To get someone like you to succumb to him gives him heightened powers."

I was trying to process everything Viktor was saying; I tried not to interrupt as I could tell he was in a hurry, so I let him continue to speak.

"Once I knew Jacob was here in your perfect town I had to call on Uriel, Raphael and Gabriel. As a guardian angel, I don't have the strength to fight him off on my own. In our realm, we need as many angels as we can get to fight off dark forces. Jacob is a dark angel; he knows your weaknesses, he targets them and tricks you into willing your soul to him. You had a weakness of the flesh, so he appeared to you to be totally irresistible; your perfect man. Do you remember those patients at the hospital? He appeared to them as perfect; they were weak and agreed to give themselves to him. Jacob became even more powerful after taking their souls."

'Well that kind of makes sense.'

Viktor continued. "But you my dear Michael, destined to become an angel, you are the most prized soul he could take, so he worked extra hard to get you to succumb to his charms. You trusted your instincts, displayed your strong, courageous spirit and willpower. You knew all along that something was not quite right with him. If he'd taken your soul, he would've been strong enough to banish all four of us angels.

"We weren't allowed to tell you directly what's going on, angel code and all. All we could do is hint at things and hope you would realise. We helped fill in some gaps; for example, I named your town Engle Byen; it's Norwegian for Angel Town," Viktor giggled.

"You had some friends in your human world similar to the ones you created here. We tried to fit in to get you to remember your human life so that you could move on to your calling," Raphael said.

"Yes, that's why Gabriel and I had to dress as women, it was quite fun too," Uriel laughed.

"We haven't had to act human in a long time, so we just did the best we could," Gabriel continued. "You were quite powerful without even realising what was happening; you continued to live in the moment, you had absolutely no memory of your human life. Those noises, bright lights and music you were hearing were coming from your hospital bed in the human world. We thought that anytime soon you may realise what was going on and we could finally assist you with your new destiny."

"We were all trapped here in your realm unable to leave until that piece of filth Jacob was gone." Raphael explained.

"We got word that something is going to happen any moment now, we are so happy to have been of some assistance to you. You are intuitive and strong; you will make an excellent angel," Uriel assured me.

I looked at Viktor; he appeared to be fading away.

"Well, Michael, this is it. Our paths may never cross again. Blessings to you, it's been a pleasure being your Guardian Angel, but I must go now. Goodbye Michael." Viktor kissed my forehead ever so gently and faded away completely.

My eyes began to well with tears.

'I'll miss you Viktor.'

I heard the faint sound of something like small footsteps approaching me quite fast. The footsteps got closer. Then, I saw him. Benson, the beautiful white Maltese dog I grew up with, running as fast as his little legs will carry him towards me. Then pawing at my legs, wanting me to pick him up, just like he would when I came home from school every afternoon. As I picked him up he licked the tears from my face.

'My beautiful boy has been waiting for me all these years.'

With Benson in my arms I turned and looked at the other angels, they all gave me a warm smile as they too faded away. I looked out into the street and noticed all the houses, roads and trees were also fading away as mist took over but my confusion turned to joy as I put all that had just happened aside and took a deep breath.

I began to remember fragments of my "human life" as Viktor put it. I could see the car hitting me and who was driving. I knew why I was out running late at night, how angry I had felt back then, the memories began flooding back, but it all seemed unreal somehow. I felt disconnected from the emotions, the pain, the "reality" of it all.

Then I realised none of that mattered because I now had Benson with me again. I felt that everything would be alright; I'd be okay with whatever came next...

Suddenly the muffled voices that I'd been hearing faintly in the back of my mind became crystal clear...

"Michael, it's mum, dad's here too. Paul, you go first."

"Mikey, I love you so much. We can't bear to let you live like this any longer. It's not really living to have all these wires and tubes keeping you alive. I know you would want to be set free, Mikey. It's been six months now and nothing has changed; no improvement. If you can hear me this is the saddest day of my life."

"Michael, dad and I agree with your partner, Paul; we can't let you go on like this. You should be allowed to rest my beautiful boy."

"Son, know that we all love you dearly and this isn't a choice we made easily. We will miss you so very much. Be free and fly my beautiful kind son. We love you."

I felt a hand on my chest; it radiated great warmth. It was in that moment I realised that my best mate, Dylan, was also there. I heard him say in a trembling voice, "Goodbye mate."

Tap tap, tap tap, psssst... beeeeeeeeeeee...

It was finally time for me to go.

DAVID GOLDON

Epilogue:
Colder

A heavy mist encases me, limiting the view of my surroundings. I don't feel the cold biting chill that should accompany this dark, gloomy winter's day.

I make the same journey often, how often, I don't know, time is just a word. Something piques my curiosity in this unchanging environment; something appears different.

My eyes scan the area near me and as far into the distance as I can see. I don't notice anything different. In the dead quiet of this place, I hear the crunching of gravel, footsteps. The crunching noise becomes louder and closer.

I see two figures dressed in black, a male and a female walking towards me. Gradually, through the mist, I make out the faces of the approaching couple; it's mum and dad.

I give them a limp smile which isn't acknowledged as they stand either side of me.

Standing in between them, I wrap my arms around their waists, drawing them in closer to me. In unison, we lower our heads to view the cold grey marble headstone of my twin brother, Zac.

It's then that I notice what has changed. Gold lettering 'Michael Pridemore' carved into the same cold grey marble headstone as my brother...

DAVID GOLDON

Also available:

Book two in the ENGLE BYEN series

THE ROAD TO
ENGLE BYEN

The thrilling prequel to

ENGLE BYEN
A PLACE TO CALL HOME

DAVID GOLDON

DAVID GOLDON

BONUS

The first chapter from the next instalment in the ENGLE BYEN series.

THE ROAD TO
ENGLE BYEN
(A Prequel)

DAVID GOLDON

DAVID GOLDON

Contact:

DavidGol**dd**on@gmail.com

www.DavidGoldon.com

DAVID GOLDON

CHAPTER ONE:
The Club

"You're an angel," the rather plump Madonna impersonator lip-synced while looking directly into Michael's ice blue eyes. Embarrassed by the attention, Michael looked away breaking eye contact with the drag queen.

At almost six-foot, high cheekbones, chiselled jaw and a well-toned muscular body, Michael had model good looks. He would often attract the attention of men, women and drag queens as well, wherever he went.

As the music faded and the drag queen left the stage, the thump-thump of loud dance music filled the club. The crowd surrounding him began to disperse, many club-goers making their way directly to the bar. Michael remained standing in the same spot glancing over to the queue at the bar waiting for it to thin out before heading over for his usual lemon lime and bitters.

"Hey, I think Flab-donna has the hots for you, she couldn't keep her eyes off you," came a voice from behind Michael. He turned around to see a short old man smiling at him.

"Yeah, I noticed she kept looking and singing at me, I didn't know where to look," Michael laughed.

"What brings a handsome young man like yourself to a dingy club like this? Are you waiting for your boyfriend to arrive?" the old guy asked.

"I don't have a boyfriend, I just finished work and came here to wind down a bit."

"Sorry, bit hard to hear, you'll have to move in closer. What do you do for a job?"

"I'm a nurse at the hospital not far from here, I often pop into this club for a while, have a drink, a bit of a dance and then go home," Michael replied in the loudest voice he could muster without screaming at the old guy.

"Never alone I'm sure, you're such a gorgeous hunk," the old guy said as he grabbed Michael on the arse and squeezed.

Usually, up for a genuine chat with new people of any age, Michael turned and walked away without saying anything to the old guy. He hated that he can't have a conversation with someone without there being an ulterior motive.

The queue at the bar had thinned and Michael maneuvered his way over to it through the throng of sweaty clubbers. The Muscle Mary behind the bar ignored the other patrons waiting for service and headed directly to Michael.

"What can I get you tonight gorgeous?" The Muscle Mary asked flashing a smile, teeth whiter than the polar ice caps.

Michael's eyes scanned the tattoos on the barman's chest and arms. "Lemon, lime and bitters, thanks."

As the barman turned around to prepare his drink, Michael couldn't help but notice the barman's tight denim shorts and pert bubble butt. Taking a five dollar note out of his wallet and holding it out in readiness for the barman to take, the barman squeezed Michael's hand shut, gave him a big smile, handed him his drink and moved on to the next customer.

Standing near the dance floor, drink in hand, Michael admired the muscled torso's dripping in sweat and moving in unison to the beat of the dance music. His favourite dance anthem of all time began to thump out of the speakers. Quickly placing his unfinished drink on the nearby ledge, he moved onto the dance floor and began moving his body to the pulsating rhythm. Wide-eyed men stared at him; wet hair, faces dripping with sweat.

He felt hands on his hips, his t-shirt moving up his stomach, he raised his arms up in the air allowing his t-shirt to be taken off by a stranger dancing behind him. The stranger tucked Michael's t-shirt into the back of his designer jeans, he turned around and smiled at the handsome young stranger, who is also shirtless, and they danced together until the song ended.

Finding himself in the middle of the dance floor covered in sweat and extremely parched, he navigated his way through the masses of bodies to get back and finish that much-needed drink. He picked up his half-full glass and guzzled down the refreshing beverage. He turned away from the dance floor, making his way to the bar, his shoes slightly sticking to the carpet. He needed water and fast.

Suddenly, Michael felt uncontrollably dizzy, his legs felt like jelly, he feared his legs were about to give way. Knowing he wouldn't be able to make it to the bar without falling over, his eyes scanned the room for somewhere to sit down. He spied a vacant barstool near a wall and made his way to it, stumbling slightly.

Now seated, he couldn't feel his legs, his arms felt numb as the *thump, thump* of the dance music invaded his head. As a thick fog of dry ice pumped into the club, the old guy with the roving hands appeared as if by magic right in front of him as he tried to steady himself by leaning against the wall.

"You all right there mate? You had too much to drink?" The old guy asked as he rubbed Michael's leg with his wrinkly old hand.

Michael tried to speak but was unable; he could hardly move; his heart began racing as he realised he had obviously been drugged. The old guy put his arm around the back of Michael's neck gently rubbing it.

"Let's get you home, I'll take good care of you," he whispered.

"Fuck off, you dirty old letch!" A loud voice came out of nowhere as the old man released his grip on Michael and went tumbling back against the wall sliding down it and landing on the sticky carpet. Virtually incapacitated and unable to speak, Michael saw the guy that assaulted the old guy. He also noticed two big burly bouncers pushing their way through the crowd over to him after witnessing the violent confrontation that had just unfolded.

"Are you with him?" one of the bouncers asked the violent hero.

"Yeah, I am, this old guy was sleazing onto my boyfriend and wouldn't take no for an answer. Sorry, but I had to do something to stop him."

"Yeah, well you and your boyfriend, who's not looking so good, better leave now." The other bouncer was helping the old guy up off the floor sitting him down on a nearby barstool.

The violent hero took Michael's t-shirt out from the back of his jeans and put it back on him. The bouncer assisted lifting Michael up off the barstool and escorted him out to the front of the club with help from the violent hero.

DAVID GOLDON

Coming November 2018:

Book three in the ENGLE BYEN series

ENGLE BYEN OPPORTUNITIES

The thrilling follow up to

THE ROAD TO ENGLE BYEN

DAVID GOLDON

DAVID GOLDON

ENGLE BYEN
OPPORTUNITIES

DAVID GOLDON

Book three in the ENGLE BYEN series

AvaOrionMedia.com

DAVID GOLDON

BONUS

ENGLE BYEN short story by

DAVID GOLDON

The Witch Next Door

DAVID GOLDON

THE WITCH NEXT DOOR

DAVID GOLDON

DAVID GOLDON

The Witch Next Door

An ENGLE BYEN *short story by*

DAVID GOLDON

DAVID GOLDON

Cover Image by Reinhard Tiburzy /shutterstock.com

Contact:

DavidGol**dd**on@gmail.com

www.DavidGoldon.com

DAVID GOLDON

Karen placed a shovel next to her overnight bag in the back of her car, slammed the boot shut and smiled. She was looking forward to what the future would hold.

* * *

Growing weary after being on the road for so long, she sighed with relief as she passed the welcome sign to the coastal town she grew up in. She was almost at her destination after the tiring drive from Melbourne.

Gently tapping her brakes, she slowed as she rounded the bends in the road leading into the town centre. She was greeted with rows of shops to her left and her right, then there it was; the ocean.

Karen did a U-turn at a set of traffic lights and drove into a car park facing the ocean. Getting out of the car, she stretched her legs, breathing in a large lungful of fresh ocean air, and then another. The sun was shining on this cold winter's morning. People were walking along the beach; some with dogs, some with children.

After feeling refreshed from the drive, she knew what she had to do before nightfall. But firstly, she wanted to visit the house she grew up in. She didn't know if it was still there, it had been at least forty years since her last visit.

Back in the car, she drove slowly through the town centre looking at the shops. Now mostly all unfamiliar to her, she only recognised a few from their unchanged shop fronts. Karen drove up over the hill, past a few

DAVID GOLDON

streets and began recognising a few houses from her childhood. She slammed the brakes on almost passing her old home. Sitting in the car, she observed the house, then turned her head to see the ocean opposite the house. She'd finally made it.

When she was ten years old, she promised herself that once she reached an age where she became old, frail and in pain, just like her suffering grandma, she would return home to regain her youth. Looking in the rear-view mirror, she observed her heavily wrinkled face and baggy eyes. Her gnarled fingers were in pain from arthritis due to holding onto the steering wheel throughout the long drive.

Smiling, she was filled with joy to observe how well maintained the house was; the new occupants must love it as much as she and her siblings had. The beautiful old house remained intact; the wrap-around porch, large front windows, even the two-seater swing on the porch looked to be the original.

Getting out of the car, she put a warm jacket on. Karen leaned against the side of the car mesmerised by the house.

Overcome with nostalgia she drifted back in time. The apple tree was still in the front yard; she could see herself swinging on an old tyre her father had secured to the tree. Her older sister pushing her while her younger brother was up in the tree picking apples and throwing them down to their father. The screen door banged as her mother emerged from the house making her way over to them. She could hear her mother's soft, gentle voice saying she was going to be making the most delicious apple pie for them tonight. Karen could smell the apple pie baking in the oven, as a tear slowly made its way down her cheek. Memories long forgotten flowed to the forefront of her mind, just like the waves of the ocean across from the house.

She suddenly recalled the neighbour's house right next door. As she shifted to gaze in search of it, she realised it was gone. Probably long since demolished by the amount of long grass that was rooted in its place.

The witch's house was no more. And the witch, who knew?

Another nostalgic flashback, Karen saw herself as a ten-year-old girl. She was wearing her favourite cherry print dress, long white socks and bright red sandals. She was creeping around outside the witch's house being extremely careful not to be seen by the witch. The witch's house had the paint peeling off the weatherboard exterior, the garden overgrown with long weeds topped with pretty yellow flowers.

As a young Karen scooted down the side of the house into the backyard, she crouched down on full alert for any sign of the old witch. All was quiet, so she made her way to the back veranda of the house. A black cat ran passed her and she let out a scream. Now the witch would surely know that Karen was there.

Karen scurried for cover hiding behind some wooden tea chests. She had heard from the kids at school that if the witch doesn't eat you she will turn you into a black cat and you would live with her forever. Karen then wondered if maybe she used to know whoever was now that black cat.

Lying in wait, everything was quiet, so perhaps the witch wasn't home after all. Karen crept away slowly from her hiding spot and made her way to the back door of the house. She gently lifted the latch on the door cautiously opening it. Poking her head in the door, there was no sign of the witch.

Karen went inside and found herself in the kitchen. She saw a metal tray on top of the stove; there were shapes of brown people on it. Her heart beat faster at the thought of the people the witch had turned brown and was about to put in her oven.

If she gets out of this house alive, she will have to tell all the kids at school about what she had seen. Would the kids at school believe that she had actually been inside the witch's house? Probably not. Unless she could take something from the house to prove that she had indeed been in there.

She saw a notebook on the kitchen table. On the cover of the notebook was written Witches Spells. Without a second thought, Karen scooped up the notebook in her small hands and ran out the back door as fast as she could back to the safety of her house next door.

Once she reached her front yard, she hid the notebook inside the front flap of her dress and walked casually back into the house and upstairs to her bedroom. Looking out of her bedroom window she checked to make sure the witch hadn't followed her back home to get her spell book back. Pulling down the blind two inches from the bottom, to allow just enough sunlight through and not be seen by the witch, she removed the notebook from her dress and opened it up on her bed. She flipped through various pages.

Most of the words she could read. There were spells on how to turn children into cats or birds, how to find love and how to stay young forever. Karen glanced at that particular spell. Maybe, she could cast that spell on her grandmother? Her Gran was old and frail and in a lot of pain. The spell involved having to stand in the ocean and recite an incantation over and over again.

She knew she would never be able to get her old gran across the dirt road, through the sand in her wheelchair and then into the ocean. But she thought, one day she will be old and frail herself and, if she could cast the spell herself before she needs a wheelchair, she will be able to walk through the sand and into the ocean and never end up like her dear old granny.

Karen hatched a plan; she would keep the witch's spell book hidden until she needed it and then she would use the spell on herself. But where would she hide the book, she won't need it for a long, long time yet. Carefully earmarking that page, she placed the book under her mattress until she could think of somewhere safer to hide it for her future, and from the witch next door.

"Karen, Karen," she could hear her mother's voice calling her from downstairs. Joyfully she made her way down the staircase and into the kitchen. It was afternoon tea time. The table had been laid out beautifully as usual. A teapot with a green and yellow striped knitted cosy took pride of place in the centre of the table surrounded by cake and treats. Karen sat in her usual chair and was joined by her parents, brother and sister at the table. Suddenly Karen squealed as her mother placed a small brown person on her plate.

Her family laughed at her. Her mother explained that the nice old lady, Wendy, from next door had dropped by a few minutes ago and gave them to her. Refusing to eat it her mother went to the cupboard and returned with a biscuit tin. Karen took the last biscuit from the tin and asked her mother if she could have the empty tin.

Ten-year-old Karen stood atop a sand dune, red plastic spade in one hand, the witch's spell book safely inside the biscuit tin in her other hand. She surveyed the wide-open beach, waves loudly crashing down, wind blowing her mousey brown hair across her face. She turned and looked back at her house, aligning herself with the front door, she took ten steps sidewards to the right, across the top of the sand dune, and decided this is where she would bury the witches spell book.

She dug a hole to the depth of the spade. Looking at the bright coloured parrot embossed on the biscuit tin, she said, "See you again when I am an old lady," and filled in the hole.

Karen's legs were weary after spending all that time propped up against her car reminiscing about her childhood and the witch next door. She hobbled over to the boot and opened it. Sunset was fast approaching. She opened up her overnight bag and took out a white cotton nightgown. She remembered she needed to wear this for the spell to work. There had not been a soul around the whole time she was parked out the front of her old home. Feeling comfortable enough, she changed into her nightgown. Grasping the shovel in her arthritic hand, she slammed the boot shut.

Hobbling across the now bitumen road dressed in only a white cotton nightgown she was freezing cold. Lining up the front door of the house she stood on top of a sand dune, took ten small side steps to the right, knelt down on the sand and began digging.

As a ten-year-old she recalled how easy it must have been to dig a hole in the sand, now many, many years later it was so painful. The sun was slowly disappearing; she had to find the tin fast. After each painful shovelful of sand was shifted, she wondered whether if it was still even there. Maybe someone else had found it and used the eternally youthful spell on themselves?

The shovel hit something. Furiously, like a dog digging up a bone, she used her hands digging up more sand until she saw it. The parrot on the biscuit tin was looking up at her as if to say, "Well, there you are."

Tears came streaming down her face as she retrieved the tin from the sand. Brushing the sand off the embossed tin parrot, she smiled. Finally, with the help of the witch's spell, she would be free of all the pain old age has brought her.

Struggling to open the tin for some time, it eventually opened. The title of the notebook, Witches Spells was as clear as the day a ten-year-old Karen placed it there for safe keeping. As she flicked through the pages, the page that was earmarked sprang open.

Dusk had begun its descent and Karen had to act fast before it was too dark to see the spell. Putting her glasses on she read the spell. Luckily, she remembered she had to wear a white cotton gown for the spell to work; she also had to wade out into the ocean up to neck height and recite the incantation written in the book, once for every year of her age. Once that was complete her youthfulness would be returned, and she could emerge from the ocean with pain becoming a distant memory. "Well, youthfulness, here I come!" Karen said to herself.

Taking off her glasses and leaving them on the sand dune with the spell book and the biscuit tin, Karen walked slowly toward the ocean. Huge waves were crashing; the squalling wind blew her long grey hair into her face. Unperturbed, freezing cold and legs almost giving way to the pain, she made it to the water's edge. Water lapped at her feet and she made her way into the rough sea.

She began repeating the incantation over and over as the water became deeper and deeper, colder and colder. Night had set in; she could no longer see the shore. Using the remainder of her strength to keep her head above water she recited her last incantation.

All the pain had gone. She felt a new strength, the strength and vigour of youth. She knew the spell of the witch next door would work and it did! Karen felt light, happy and free as she slowly made her way back to the shore.

Oddly, the sun began to shine again. Maybe she had been out there in the cold ocean for longer than she'd thought. Surely not that long. The water wasn't cold anymore. She continued wading through the water and the waves, her white nightdress clinging to her body.

A mirror, yes, she must find a mirror to see if her face was as youthful as her body felt. The water was only knee deep now, not long to reach the shore.

Her eyes caught sight of a white object lying at the water's edge. Karen emerged from the water and made her way to the object. It was a body. The seemingly lifeless body of an old woman wearing a white cotton nightgown.

Karen immediately recognised the face of the old woman. It was her!

She looked up and saw a young, blonde man standing over her lifeless body. He looked up at her and smiled. "Hi Karen, I'm Viktor. Welcome to Engle Byen," he said in a strange accent.

Karen looked at him in total confusion...

DAVID GOLDON

DAVID GOLDON
Author Talk NOW ON-LINE

View this fascinating Author Talk now at:
AvaOrionMedia.com/Events/
Or search ▶️ **YouTube** *for:* **Ava Orion Media**

About The Author

David attended a newly formed writing group to support his friends. He had no intention, patience or time to write any stories himself, or so he thought. Inadvertently he was drawn into participating in some writing exercises. His long-cobwebbed creativity began to emerge transitioning into a new-found passion for story writing. David aims to infiltrate the LGBT literary world with stories of love, life and lessons learned with an Australian flavour.

David lives in Melbourne, Australia with his long-term partner and two fur babies.

www.DavidGoldon.com

DAVID GOLDON

DAVID GOLDON

*Have you ever dreamt of holding your own
published book in your hands?*

AVA ORION Media
can make that self-publishing dream come true!

We also help with smaller work like written content
for websites, blogs, essays and so forth. If you're
finding it challenging to determine the appropriate
spelling, grammar or how to effectively express what
you want to say... we would love to help you!

So email: info@AvaOrionMedia.com now!

~

I never had bedtime stories read to me as a child.
I never read books as a child, but some things are
meant to be... some passions are in our DNA,
they travel with us through lifetimes
and nothing can hold them down.
So now I love to read, more than that, I LOVE
proofreading, editing and writing.
I would love to read your stories, that's always an
exciting adventure for me, and then I'll help you put
your best words forward...

Michael Young
Founder ~ Ava Orion Media

I believe in the power of our words.

www.AvaOrionMedia.com
www.MichaelYoungAuthor.com

▶ **YouTube** *Search:* **Ava Orion Media**

DAVID GOLDON